THE LION IN THE THICKET

WILL TOLAR

 LUCIDBOOKS

CHAPTER 1

"Hello," a voice yelled from the threshold of Paul Schaffer's front door. Paul blinked his eyes and flexed his fingers as the computer stared back at him.

"Yes," Paul said, leaning around the corner of his home office, one hand on a pistol.

"Hey, man! Don't shoot!" His best friend, Todd, laughed as he came through the front door, hands in the air and a smile on his face. The front door opened right into the living room and Todd placed his hat and phone on a coffee table by the door.

"Todd, what are you doing here?" Paul asked. "Are there any more flowers or cards there?"

"Um," Todd reopened the front door and checked outside as his friend requested. "Nothing that I see." A car passed and honked and Todd waved half-heartedly. "Wait, there's a small box," Todd said. He shut the door and re-entered with the package, a small box. "Dang dude, do you ever clean up?" Todd asked jokingly while he grabbed with his spare hand a few bags of fast food, that the gnats had found and placed them in the kitchen trash. "It smells like fast food and feet up in here."

Paul rolled his eyes while he walked into plain sight and leaned against the countertop of his kitchen. "You can put that box on the table there and…. what are you doing here at lunchtime?" Paul asked, glancing at the clock.

"Just stopping by," Todd responded, moving the clutter before setting the box down on the kitchen table. "A good maid will clean your house for about $50." Todd glanced at the curtain-covered windows. "A little sunlight never hurt anybody, Paul," Todd joked a little while he looked at the mess that was Paul Schaffer's home. That is when he spotted the bottle. "Drinking alone may not be good for you either."

"Sara and I used to drink wine on a lot of occasions, but since…" Paul stopped and quickly walked over to the counter, put the wine away, and washed out the glasses. Todd waited in silence. He didn't want to upset Paul in any way. "Did that order of gaskets and bolts get out to Germany?" Paul asked while Todd lingered and stared at the refrigerator covered in pictures of Paul's life. Todd's eyes began to burn as tears ran down his face.

"Paul, that was nine months ago," he said and wiped the tears with his shirt. He attempted to pick up a few more things while he listened to what was going on in his friend's life. Paul enjoyed visitors but did not like all the pity, and Todd knew better than to joke about Paul and his pajamas at noon. "I'm sorry for everything you've been through." Todd cleared his throat and gave his friend a much-needed hug.

"Do you want some coffee?" Paul moved a few baby bottles that had dried next to the coffee cups and found Todd's cup. He poured Todd a cup of coffee and set it on the bar area next to the kitchen.

"Where's Jackson?" Todd asked curiously.

"My mom came by and wanted to keep him for the rest of the day, so I could try and get some sleep." Paul yawned before he rudely addressed his friend. "Dude, why are you here?" Paul asked as the steam from the coffee settled around his face.

Todd adjusted the coffee cup in his hand and waited, his words needed to be thought about first. "The board announced changes today, and Gary had me take up a collection for you, the warehouse guys contributed the most." Todd smiled half-heartedly and took a seat in the living room. His eyes were still watery and red. "I need you to sit for a minute, please Paul." He began gently and placed an envelope on the coffee table.

Paul stood silently in the kitchen; he knew that Todd was about to give him some bad news.

"Paul, I know life has been tough on you. Hell, most men would have given up, and well, there's no other way to say this. Todd paused, avoiding Paul's eyes. He stood, and ran a hand through his hair. "The board of advisors approved two months of paid leave for you to recover. In their eyes, that was enough time to bury her and move on. But it's been seven months since your wife passed, Paul." He splayed his arms out, compassion in his eyes.

"You gotta be kidding me!" Paul hollered out. "A Board of snakes." Paul raised his voice. "So, they couldn't fire me themselves, so they sent you," Paul asked.

"They paid you two more months than what was agreed on," Todd said, keeping his voice steady. "You haven't returned; so you're being replaced. I'm sorry to say this! I volunteered to tell you. I thought it would be better coming from a friend," Todd sat back down, hoping to project calm to his friend. Paul just stared at the wall.

"Pay? I wasn't paid for any leave. I have been living off my savings. I gave that company ten years." Paul shook his head and mumbled under his breath. "How much money have I made them? Millions!" He popped his knuckles.

Todd spoke again, voice low and soothing, "In the end, we're all just a number on a payroll." Todd put his cup in the sink.

"I will wash it," Paul said, and Todd stepped back, nodding. "You know fifty dollars is not a lot for a clean house." Paul looked around and tapped his finger against that coffee cup.

"Come over to my place this weekend. We're having a big cookout. Girls in bikinis. My cellar is full of wine," Todd grinned. Paul gave him a look. "Get out of this house, this town, and enjoy yourself. Go find you a rebound for the weekend. Just don't run off and get married yet," Todd added.

"My pink slip?" Paul asked.

"Don't worry about that. It'll be delivered by mail in a few days."

Todd tapped his finger on the envelope. "Nine hundred and forty-eight bucks. Book a cruise now to anywhere you want. When you come back, let's find you a job." He stuck out his hand for Paul to shake, and Paul hesitated, then met him halfway.

"My house this weekend. We have a spare room with your name on it. Girls in bikinis!" Todd adjusted his expensive shades and moved forward to grab Paul with a bear hug. "People, fresh air. Get out and have fun." Todd turned to walk to the front door and passed by the dinner table, which was piled with gifts left by friends and strangers. "Dude, you are loved." Todd looked curiously at the new package from earlier, with no stamp or return address. It was a small box, with the words Papa loves you.

"And, who is Papa?" Todd read the writing on the box from that morning.

"I don't have a clue," Paul shrugged.

Todd grinned. "Probably, an old lover of yours that heard you were single." Paul forced a chuckle and cracked a smile.

"Go to work. I'll see you this weekend," Paul said and swiped at Todd with the broom.

Todd laughed and jumped back, hands in the air. He moved towards the front door, stopped, and held the handle. "If I could take your place, you know I would."

"You're a terrible liar. Besides, you would've already killed yourself by now," Paul quipped. The two men stood for a moment; Todd hated to see his friend like this. "I will see you this weekend."

Paul gently escorted his friend out the door and retreated to his room. He pondered the idea of moving on but he knew he was not ready to let go. Everything in this house reminded him of his beloved Sara. If Paul could talk to her about getting over her, then maybe.

Sara's grave was just a few minutes down the road. It was the only place Paul visited anymore. As he pulled into the cemetery, the gravel under the tires made a distinct noise, just a little different from the main highway.

Applewhite Cemetery was a popular place to lay to rest many loved ones.

Paul was not sure of the age of the cemetery, but vines covered a majority of the sign.

Paul pulled into his usual parking spot. This evening, before the sun went down, he decided to visit her for just a few minutes. From his car, Sara's tombstone was in sight. Paul breathed deeply, like their first date.

Today, he sat in the Land Rover a little longer than normal. Paul hoped he could daydream about her. It was a suicide move. Memories of her sometimes haunted him rather than helped. Paul wanted to tell Sara about losing his job. He knew it was weird, but they talked about everything.

Paul could still see her, sitting beside him, riding the back roads for hours. He kept her sunglasses next to him just like old times. He hoped the door would open, and she would hop right in where she belonged.

"God, can I have one more minute with her, to say goodbye? That's all I ask. Help me let go," Paul wept and reached for the pistol.

A tap on his window startled him. A little Hispanic man with a giant smile waved. Paul, stared for a second, then realized what just happened and stashed the pistol under the seat and lowered his window.

"Señor, the gates close in an hour," he said.

"Oh, okay, do you work here?" Paul asked. His heart felt warm suddenly, as the little man talked.

"My Father asked me to look after them here. So, I check the property," he said.

Applewhite was a big cemetery, but to keep someone here at all hours seemed ridiculous and costly. "So, you're here all the time?" Paul asked.

"When my father asks me, I stay longer," the man shrugged.

The grounds always looked well taken care of, but someone could mow and weed eat in a day. Not an all-day kind of job, at least Paul thought.

"My name's Paul," he said, avoiding the man's eyes.

"Immanuel," the man responded. "We know you."

Paul smiled, a little confused, but turned to face Sara's grave.

"Yes, we have been watching over that one." The worker said with pride.

Paul locked his Land Rover, and they shook hands as men do.

"I'll lock the front gate if I stay too long," Paul offered, hoping the worker would grant him privacy with his wife.

Immanuel's face seemed to shine, even though the evening sun had begun to disappear behind the pine trees.

"You seem harmless," Paul said but he turned and retrieved his pistol from his vehicle. "I just like to keep it on me," Paul explained himself. He put the pistol in his waistband.

"My friend, no harm here. The dead know nothing," Immanuel said.

"Thanks," Paul waved and quickly turned away.

CHAPTER 2

"I got here as quick as I could," Paul stopped just a few feet from Sara's grave. Paul made an attempt to look more presentable to his beloved. He straightened his back and fixed the scruffy mess that sat on top of his head and face. He tried to pull himself together.

The tombstone is set about fifty yards from the entrance and straight back to the edge of the property, then to the right. Paul purchased both plots at the same time. The cemetery was open. The only tree was beside their grave plots and the shade was nice in the evening. The cemetery was always free of trash, and the workers kept the grass cut well.

The fence behind her grave was down, the aluminum frame was bent, dragged, and then flattened. The dark thicket was easily noticeable. Paul shook his head and turned to face Sara's grave again, disgusted. "Why would they leave that open? Stupid Mexican will let anybody in here." Paul spit on the ground and glanced around the cemetery for Immanuel. What he saw, was not Immanuel, but deep claw marks on the only tree that gave Paul shade.

He rubbed his fingers over the marks; the tree bleed moisture. He faced the thicket in wonder at what really was going on in that present moment. "The same marks on the tree...are on this fence," Paul said as he kneeled down like a hunter scouting his animal.

He remembered the first time he laid eyes on the thicket. It'd been the day of the funeral. Paul was certain he heard a roar of some type come from the darkness of the thicket. His heart leaped within briefly, but the sea of faces that day never looked up to pay tribute. The preacher never stopped talking.

Paul touched the pistol in his waistband before returning to Sara's grave. The fresh dirt had created a nice bed of grass instead. He rubbed his fingers through the grass in hopes of touching her hand. Paul tossed the grass in the air. The pain that he could not let go of gripped him like electricity. He glanced around the cemetery, but no one else was around. He cleaned his face. The more he talked to her, the more his eyes watered the ground he knelt on. He beat his fist against the ground. He clutched his chest as thoughts of her perfume and her body ran through his mind. All it took was just a thought of her, a piece of what was taken away from him, and the blackness began to set in.

Thunder cracked the air overhead and brought Paul back to reality. The dark thicket shook and the birds flew and a herd of deer ran out into the open cemetery only to jump a fence and scatter to and fro in the twilight hours of the day. Paul looked past his wife's tombstone, unaware of what really just happened. He glared into the unknown and wondered what could have made that noise. To his surprise the thicket shook again, accompanied by a roar.

"What the…" Paul gripped his pistol for security, his eyes now focused on the thicket. Something was running back and forth as limbs and twigs snapped. Paul's heart beat against his ribcage

He stood; the pistol gripped firmly at his side. He wiped the sweat from his eyes and gulped. Around him, the air was still and silent.

"Hello," Paul called, his voice cracking ever so slightly. Nothing.

"Who's there?" He called again, voice louder and steadier this time. He bent forward never taking his eyes off the thicket in front of him and picked up a rock. He threw it into the little wilderness and it struck the ground with a thud. Paul bravely stepped closer to the thicket.

The trees shook violently again. His stomach clenched painfully. He backed away slowly.

Suddenly, like a door, the thicket parted, and a blur of tan fur bounded towards him. He blinked, and the breath left his lungs, he yelled, stumbling back, and landed on the hard ground. He fumbled with the gun and tried to get back to his feet.

Desperate, Paul pointed his pistol towards this beast from the thicket, and the beast paused and paced sideways. It roared.

"A lion," Paul muttered, a hysterical laugh escaping his throat. It lunged forwards nipping at Paul's feet, then backed away just as quickly. Paul scrambled back, and the lion lunged again, grabbing at Paul's legs as if to drag him into the wilderness from which he'd emerged. Paul kicked at the beast, still steadying his pistol, Paul's heart was beating hard; fire was in his lungs. The lion swatted the open air with his giant paws, slapped the ground next to Paul, and swatted the pistol into the abyss. The lion stood in front of him, poised to pounce.

"No," Paul yelled, throwing his arms up in surrender. The lion stopped its assault as the dust settled around Paul, who lowered his arms and met the beast's eyes. The roar that was so frightening before, seemed much calmer, almost a huff as the lion sat down on his back haunches breathing heavily. Paul sat back and gasped a breath of air, as the lion's tail swished back and forth.

After an eternity, the lion stood, turned back to the thicket, and paced towards it. The bushes opened as if to greet it, and just before it walked back through, it turned to look at Paul again. It huffed again at Paul before the thicket closed behind it.

Paul stood up quickly admired his torn pants and stepped towards the thicket, only to stop. He wanted adventure to break his routine. A wave of dizziness washed over him, and the world around him faded into black. The last thing he registered was his body meeting the hard ground. Then he knew no more.

– – – –

"Honey, it's time," Sara said, holding her purse at the front door, taking deep breaths, and holding her belly. Paul was a complete mess; a kid who was about to be a father.

"Just trying to find my keys," he said and grabbed the television remote instead. "Dang it." By the front door, Sara checked her pulse and blood pressure with her fingers. "Sara, that is only going to make it worse," Paul suggested, but she never listened to him.

"It is high, but the Doctor will know what to do." Sara looked at Paul. "Our son is waiting and so is the hospital."

Paul finally found his keys and grabbed his overnight bag.

"Ok, now we're ready." He opened the front door and ushered his wife to the car.

"Paul, don't kill us before we get to the hospital! It's raining." Sara took big breaths of air.

Paul did his best and gripped the wheel a little tighter. He only managed to run a few red lights and he ignored only one stop sign.

"Record time!" Paul said while Sara just glared. Once inside the hospital, they were escorted to a hospital room and in short order, Sara was changed into a gown and nurses had her hooked to several monitors. One nurse checked her vitals and even did a quick ultrasound to check on little Jackson.

"The Doctor will be here in just a minute." The nurse asked Paul to take a seat as he paced around the room.

"Sara, how are you doing?" Paul held her hand and kissed her forehead.

"My contractions are pretty intense," she said and looked around the room. Tears were in her eyes. "When is the doctor going to be here?" She asked.

"He is coming, probably busy right next door," Paul said looking at his wife. He brushed her hair back from her eyes.

"I am scared." Sara's lip quivered.

"Me too." Paul smiled. "You're doing great." Paul began to fan his wife with a clipboard and glanced over at the monitor Sara was hooked up to. He tensed. Her blood pressure was extremely high. He put himself between her and that monitor.

Finally, the doctor came busting into the room. "Sara, today is a big day," the doctor said. He was an older man in, his early sixties, that seemed experienced. "Doctor Tolbert," he added and glanced back at the monitor. "Dad, I need you to put these scrubs on. A nurse will come and get you in just a minute. We need to prep your wife for a quick c-section."

"Wait, what? Where's Doctor Anderson? He's our primary physician," Paul said.

"Dr. Anderson is ill. Son, just trust me," Dr. Tolbert said, reaching out and putting his hand on Paul's back. Before Paul could even think, nurses were wheeling Sara out. He tried to grab Sara's hand but wasn't quick enough.

"What's going on?" Paul yelled, but the doctor ignored him and kept on walking out. "Sara, I'm right behind you," he called but wasn't sure she heard.

"It's cold in there, so just put those scrubs over what you are wearing. Follow me please," the nurse instructed.

Paul slipped the scrubs on rather quickly. "How serious is this?" Paul and the nurse walked together down the hall.

"High blood pressure is normal; it should go down after your son is here," she said, without smiling.

In haste, the doctor ran past them in the hallway, nearly knocking Paul over. "Sorry," he yelled over his shoulder but never turned to acknowledge Paul as he disappeared behind some double doors just yards in front of them. The young nurse stopped in the hallway and grabbed Paul's arm.

"Jesus," she said.

"Is my wife ok?" Paul asked the nurse, who had begun to pray in the hallway. Paul could hear a newborn baby from behind those doors. "I was supposed to be in there!" He yelled. The nurse tried to turn Paul around and take him back to the room, but he pulled away from her.

In a brief dash, Paul placed his hands on the double doors the other doctor had just disappeared behind. He was met by a male nurse, who pushed Paul back, not letting him past the threshold of those double doors. Paul could see his wife on the operating table, and several nurses were huddled, praying in the corner of the room. He heard someone yell "clear!" as she was shocked. The male nurse pushed him back into the hallway. Paul swung his fist, knocking the guy out cold.

"Sara," Paul yelled, struggling against the bodies that now surrounded him as the high-pitched roar of a flatlined heart ripped his world completely apart.

– – – –

"Sara!" Paul shot up from the wet ground of the cemetery. Around him, night had fallen. The rain had just begun to fall and it felt nice on his face. He glanced down at the buzzing, glowing device beside him. He picked up the phone, glancing at the screen. It was Todd. He swiped to answer and put the phone to his ear.

"Hey, Bro," Todd spoke from the other side.

"What's up?" Paul said as a frog croaked.

"I was calling to check on you. Sorry, it's late, but I had you on my mind today. Are you ready to go to work?" Todd asked.

"Yeah, I'm ready," Paul hesitated but glanced at the dark shapes of headstones around him.

"Listen, a recruiter at the golf course said he was actively looking for a maintenance guy for the local nursing home. He asked me today if I knew anybody, and I thought about you," Todd said. When Paul didn't answer right away, he added, "You have to start somewhere, Paul."

"Yeah," Paul said quietly.

"Well, if you're serious, just be at the nursing home in town tomorrow at 8:00 am. I just feel like this would be a good thing for you. A new start," Todd encouraged his friend.

"I appreciate it, man," Paul replied. "Hey Todd, has the news said anything about a lion escaping or something similar to that?"

"God's not done with you yet," Todd said; then the call ended.

In the still of the night, Paul stared at his phone. He shook his head and stood. God has forgotten about me, Paul thought.

Using the light from his phone, Paul made his way back to the car, got in, and started the car. He put his head against the wheel, blew out a breath, then put the car in reverse. He slowly pulled out of his parking spot and made his way to the gates.

At the gate, Paul came to a halt. The little Hispanic man stood waiting on him, smile shining in the glow of the headlights.

"What in the world?" Paul muttered, glancing at the car's clock, it was almost 11:00 pm. Paul lowered his car window.

"I thought you were going home earlier," Paul said. "Do you have a place to go?"

The man's wrinkled face wrinkled further with his smile. "Papa is around here somewhere," he said and looked past Paul's vehicle towards that giant, dark thicket.

Paul turned, looking for another person. He sighed. "You ever had one of those days where you think somebody else is writing your story?" he asked, rubbing a hand over his wet hair.

Immanuel's face softened. "Life is better that way my friend," the man suggested and ushered Paul out of the gate. Paul smiled, put the window back up, and slowly drove out of the cemetery. He stopped at the main road and watched Immanuel in the rearview mirror. The man locked the gate, walked toward the thicket, and disappeared.

"I must be tired," he muttered, and then pulled away.

The drive home was quiet. In his head, he played the events of the evening over again. The lion, the thicket, the mysterious Immanuel. Paul found himself wanting to turn back, to follow the lion and the man into the thicket, to see what would happen. Whether it resulted in his death or not, the lion had to be much greater than where he was now in life.

Once home, Paul absent-mindedly locked up, prepared for bed, and lay awake long into the night, thinking about the lion.

CHAPTER 3

At 6:00 am his cellphone alarm rang in his back pocket. Paul stood in front of the bathroom mirror, shirtless, wondering what a maintenance guy wears. He assumed pants and a shirt that could get paint, dirt, or whatever stained on it. He had not worked in maintenance since college. He changed his shirt several times and his shoes, he only changed once, dressing down casually. He settled on a polo shirt and a pair of pants that had some miles on them but were decent. He almost thought of Sara while looking at himself in the bathroom mirror, as her medication was still in plain sight. Paul glanced at the trash can first but just closed his eyes and put her things away. "Courage, Paul. Courage."

He turned off the bathroom light and made his way to the kitchen to drink his coffee and pack a peanut butter and jelly sandwich, then gathered up what he thought he needed. No suit and tie today—just Paul. He walked out to his Land Rover and hopped in.

Paul noticed the interior had mud smeared in several places on the seat and steering wheel.

"The lion in the thicket," Paul said to himself. He thought that was a dream. But the evidence was right there in front of him now. "No one would believe this," he muttered to himself.

Paul knew for certain if that lion appeared again, he would chase him into that thicket, and face him. He felt like after all that he had been through, he needed to prove himself. He wasn't a coward, but life had taken its toll on him.

He adjusted his rearview mirror and thought about the lion's eyes. They had seemed so real, and so did the invitation into danger.

The sun was a beautiful sight on the horizon. Several of his neighbors waved. Paul smiled and raised a hand back. He tugged at his shirt collar. His phone dinged and brought him back to this present moment along with a sense of urgency to get to work.

The nursing home was not far, maybe ten miles. Paul knew of it but had never visited the building. He parked his Land Rover under some trees.

He'd arrived a little early, something he always made a habit of doing. At a glance, he noticed the grass needed to be cut and the hedges needed trimming. He would ask to do that first and try to make a good impression. For the money Paul was to be paid, he could give this place a year. In his mind, a year was enough time to get back on his feet.

He walked along the sidewalk from the parking lot that lead to the west side of the building like Todd had instructed and looked for the side entrance. The cracks in the sidewalk nearly twisted his ankle.

"You get used to it." A man smoking a cigarette laughed as Paul walked by. They both chuckled but only waved and walked past each other.

Paul's eyes were drawn to the poorly maintained landscaping that surrounded the south side of the nursing home. It was even worse further down the building. He could see fire ant mounds and a few wasp nests on the siding of the facility. There was plenty of work to be done around here.

Upon arriving at the side entrance's double doors, Paul stopped. He hadn't seen a set of the double doors since Sara died in that hospital. His heart began to race, and he could hear the blood pounding in his ears. He fought the urge to turn around and go home.

"Excuse me!"

Paul jumped and turned to find a woman behind him. She was dressed nice and modest, her hair was brown and shoulder length. One would describe her as career-driven and cute with a kind smile.

"Pardon me!" Paul said and moved aside. The woman smiled generously and walked past him. Paul forgot about those painful double doors that held him captive. This woman was nice to look at, very easy on the eyes. She held her security card up to be scanned and waited for the red light to turn green. When she got halfway through, she spun around and asked.

"May I help you?" Her eyes smiled, too.

"Um… I'm a new hire looking for the maintenance or HR department. Well, I'm new, but just a short-timer. I have bigger plans," he ran a hand through his hair and looked to the side.

She chuckled. "Down the hall, first door on your left. That's the maintenance department. Your boss should already be in there, I think. You'll get your card for security, and it will let you in and out of the side doors where there is no nurse's station. These residents like to try and escape." Then she turned and began to walk away, her heels clicking against the floor. She paused briefly, looked over her shoulder, and said, "I'll be seeing you later about some paperwork, drug testing, and our insurance plan… probably tomorrow."

"Tomorrow's Saturday," Paul smiled and followed her a few steps. "But it does feel like Monday."

"I like that sense of humor," she replied, then resumed her walk.

"Who are you?" He asked as he leaned towards her, but she turned a corner and was gone.

Paul stood on the threshold of those double doors. The automatic door was also confused as it opened and closed back and forth on his foot.

"Sir, you need to move forward or I have to hit the emergency alarm," a nurse said with a half-smile inside the building.

"Oh, yeah sorry," Paul stuttered and quickly moved to get completely inside.

Several residents, some in military attire, roamed the halls in wheelchairs. The hallway smelled faintly of urine and disinfectant. It was offensive to his senses, but the smell got more tolerable after a few moments. Quiet enveloped him as he passed by several residents. One seemed asleep in his chair, but when Paul walked by him, he felt a tug on his arm. It was just enough for Paul to stop and look at the man, who still seemed to be sleeping. Paul dismissed the event and proceeded along the hallway until he stood in front of the maintenance office.

The handle rattled loosely in his grip. "How hard is it to tighten some screws?" He mumbled.

"New guy, come on in," a voice beckoned from inside.

"I knew you would be early, so I came early." A round, scruffy little man sat behind a computer desk as Paul came fully inside the office.

"Good morning. I'm Paul, Paul Schaffer," he said and reached over the desk to shake hands.

"Terry," the man replied and gestured to a chair in front of the desk.

"Nice to meet you," Paul concluded and took his seat.

"So, Paul, I hear you need a new start. I think this is a good place for you," Terry said and paused.

"I could use it," Paul agreed. The office was small and modest with a television, microwave, and a small sink. "What do you do here?"

"I'm the supervisor," Terry replied and leaned back in his chair. He took a bite of a honeybun and chased it down with a swig of coffee. "We pretty much do everything but clean the toilets around here, so you need to be flexible to do whatever needs doing. Whatever that may be," he said, bringing his back to an upright position with a plop. His large belly jiggled a bit. "Todd recommended you. I've always respected him, so here we are," Terry said. He waved a hand around the room, grinning.

"It is just me here, or…" Paul trailed off.

"It's just you and me," Terry replied.

From the looks of what Paul had seen so far, he knew that it would be just him doing most of the physical labor.

"Most people come and go within two years. They find something better," Terry said, but Paul was distracted by a familiar clicking of heels outside the door. "Paul?"

"Sorry." Paul turned back to face Terry, not realizing he'd looked away in the first place.

"Ah," Terry began, knowingly. "That's Miss Davenport. No man has been able to snatch her up yet. I think every man in this facility, including a few residents, has tried. The mid-thirties, never been married, fit as a fiddle, and all business on her end. She stopped returning my emails," he added, rubbing his belly. "A little ungrateful, I think. What's wrong with asking a woman what type of perfume she wears? Next thing you know, you're standing before the big wigs, and they take your computer away for a month."

Terry crossed his arms, and Paul was strongly reminded of a child by the pout on a grown man's face.

Several minutes later, Miss Davenport walked by again. She met Paul's eyes and smiled before walking on. Paul shifted in his chair.

"That is odd," the fat man said.

"What is?" Paul asked, still looking out into the hallway.

"You might want to stick around because she's never walked past my door twice in one morning before work begins," Terry said, and Paul looked back over. The other man took a big bite of his honeybun, chewed, and added, "Everything she needs is in her office." He took a swig of his coffee. "Well, I have lost a little weight," he said and rubbed his belly.

Paul held back a snicker. "So, am I officially hired?" he asked.

"Yes, of course! Welcome to the family. Since it's Friday, come back on Monday at the same time, 8:00 am, and we'll get started then. I haven't had a helper in a week, and it's been a little slow. Get your mind right." Terry shuffled through his desk, then held a can of tobacco. "I haven't been getting out of my office until 10:00 am to fix anything," he whispered.

"Thank you, Terry. I'm looking forward to working with you," Paul said as he stood, holding out his hand. He hesitated, then added. "It's only fair to tell you that I do plan on getting back into management. This is not something I see doing long-term."

"I know your work history. If you just up and quit, I won't be mad. Most people do. I also know that you lost your wife recently and that you have a baby. Losing your wife and being a first-time dad all at once is hard. Take your time, son," Terry said, kindly.

"I will do my best," Paul said, a little taken back by the kind words.

"There's always someone with a sadder story than yours," Terry added as he spit into his coffee cup. His eyes were focused somewhere on Paul's lower half, and he giggled. "I see you met John Hunt."

"What?" Paul raised an eyebrow.

Terry pointed to Paul's shirt. "You've been marked, twice," he laughed softly.

Paul looked around, searching for what Terry was referring to.

Terry continued, "You only need to be worried if he marked your neck; he's just messing with you right now. The security guard here hates Mr. Hunt; he gets his neck marked several times a week."

Paul finally found something unfamiliar. "What the?" He mumbled. There was a red mark on his arm and another on his shirt. He wiped at the one on his arm.

"Red Sharpie, it stays on for a while. Take two showers," Terry chuckled and rubbed his eyes. Then he showed Paul the back of his hand, where he, too, had a red mark. "He keeps stealing markers from here and there in the facility. Not sure where he finds the red ones. Some say that old guy was a professional killer, a long time ago. Spent most of his time in Mexico and South America. Grade A man-killer."

Paul scoffed. "That old man in a wheelchair, was a contract killer? Wait, which one? There were about five in the hallway," Paul said and walked to the door to look out into the hallway. Strangely, he felt only curiosity.

"No women or kids have been marked in this facility," Terry said as he joined Paul at the door. "He talks a lot, but no one understands him. He can pick a lock in the dark, but he either has a little dementia or he's just crazy. I think cancer is killing him. He had a car wreck about a year ago and has not yet recovered his ability to walk."

Paul peeked around the corner from the office to find the hall empty. "That's sad, to die in here. Caged like an animal," He scanned from left to right. "Where did everyone go?"

Terry checked the time. "Breakfast for the residents, so I have another thirty minutes on my break." He walked back to his desk, sat, and propped his feet up, then pulled his cap down over his eyes.

Paul rolled his eyes and reminded himself this was only temporary and gave a lazy wave before exiting the office completely.

Paul knew that he would not be working here long. "I will see you Monday." Terry hardly looked but did give a wave as Paul left the room, he was more concerned about wiping those crumbs from his mouth. "That old man is harmless," Terry said as Paul shut the door behind him.

The empty hall stretched before him. With people, it had been silent. Empty, it was like a tomb. Near the exit, Paul found an elderly man in a wheelchair, looking at something through the window, deep in concentration. Suddenly, he let out a chuckle and tapped the window. "I see you. Where have you been?" The old man asked, still looking outside.

Paul leaned against the wall, arms and legs crossed, head cocked to the side. The old man continued to stare outside, occasionally tapping the glass and chuckling again. Paul saw an abandoned cup nearby, inched off the wall, and picked it up.

"Did you bring Papa with you?" the old man asked. Paul looked a little closer and realized the man was talking to, not his reflection, but a black butterfly that rested on the glass window. The old man did not look like someone who roamed the halls and marked his victims with stolen red Sharpies. He was a big guy, with a greying face and beard. Paul imagined he was probably much bigger and stronger thirty years ago.

Paul, the cup still in hand, moved forward.

"Excuse me, may I use this trash can?" Paul asked.

The old man turned to face Paul, and a red Sharpie fell to the ground. Paul's eyes widened, as did the old man's. He looked like a kid who had been caught with his hand in the cookie jar.

"So, you're John Hunt?" Paul asked, leaning around the man to put the cup in the trash.

"Do I know you?" the old man asked. Paul lifted his arm to reveal the red mark.

"Oh!" John chuckled. "I get bored around here, not much to do."

Paul couldn't find it in himself to be angry at this man whose kind eyes and gentle smile invited him to stay. He smiled back and reached a hand forward.

Paul introduced himself, cautiously. "I am the new maintenance helper, I start Monday," Paul said.

"New guy with big plans, but may I see your hands?" John asked. Paul agreed and showed him his hands. "Soft, not even a scar on these baby mittens." John rubbed his chin. "Grace is when we get to start over." He spoke slowly as someone taught him. "You do not fit here, do you?"

"I was in sales and parts distribution. I drive a Land Rover," Paul said and shook his head. "I sat at the king's table once and now I am here begging for crumbs."

"The last man I killed drove a Land Rover." John interrupted Paul who failed to reply but slowly returned his hand to his side, just a little cautious. Paul glanced down the hall and hoped Miss Davenport would come back around the corner and break up the awkwardness he felt. Paul would have liked to see her again before he left.

"What would you do, if a lion just jumped out of the mess of limbs and bushes there?" John asked. The old man pointed his finger into the hedge of overgrown bushes, weeds, and mystery.

"Um…" Paul hesitated quietly.

"You could live a thousand lifetimes and it may never happen." His voice trembled; his lip quivered in emotion. "I never felt more alive in all my years. To run with a lion; God I beg of you for one more chance!" John exclaimed and looked up to the ceiling. "My legs are not strong anymore, but my heart is ready."

Deep down inside Paul regretted not chasing that lion yesterday. The more they conversed, the more Paul felt connected to this old warrior.

The old man politely turned back toward Paul. "You stayed to listen as I spoke of the lion in the thicket. Most people just walk away or ignore my mumbling." He said. Their eyes locked in a quick gaze, both wanted to know more about each other. John leaned forward in his wheelchair and smelled the air where they stood. "I do not smell the lion on you." John shuffled his wheelchair and noticed the bump on Paul's head. "I smell fear." He pushed himself away from Paul.

He was right, Paul was terrified. "So, you chased after the lion?" He directed everything towards this old man.

"Yes, of course, he called to me from his dwelling place. We had a good fight many years ago." John sat up in his chair and pointed his finger toward Paul, like a lightbulb being turned on. "Did a little Hispanic man offer you any bread and wine yet?"

"No!" Paul shook his head rather peculiarly.

"Dang, well it may be different for others," John thought aloud.

"So, when did you get offered the bread and wine?" Paul looked around the corner to see if anyone listened to their conversation.

"Let's see, how did it all start for me? It has been many years." John rubbed his chin again. "Oh, I was shot to pieces in Mexico, bleeding in the valley just about to be overrun... I can hear the dogs barking now, coming for me, behind them their masters are cheering in Spanish as my blood trail is getting easier to find in the dark of night."

The old man's pupils shined as he motioned with his hands and glanced around the room for cover, he even broke a leaf off a plant to hide behind. "You might want to pull up that chair," John said. Subconsciously, Paul was so desperate for answers, that he already seated himself with a chair he found in the hallway.

"Go on." Paul bumped John's leg with the back of his hand.

"I was betrayed, somebody wanted my head." John's eyes widened.

"Who would want you dead?" Paul asked.

"Lycan!" John exclaimed. "He was born in Russia, some said raised by wolves, hunted with the pack eating raw meat, walked on all fours and he killed his first man when he was only a boy." John Hunt took the Sharpie from his pocket and began to slash the air around him, defensively. "He was a monster, fierce and barbaric. He was bigger than me, more experienced, and had no standards to hunt by, he would kill women and children. If there was one man I feared upon this earth, it would be that monster." John paused.

"So, what happened?"

"Forgive me," John chuckled. "I rarely get visitors who listen to my babbling. I was busted up bad in Mexico, barely clinging to consciousness. The dogs were almost upon me as I tried to get to higher ground to take a defense position. My lungs were on fire, I could now hear the paws of the dogs running toward me when a little Hispanic man just walks up behind me in the darkness and places his arms around me, and picks me up. My energy was low because I had lost so much blood."

"Were you shot?" he asked.

"Um, yes, twice, but it is what happened next that I need you to listen to. Maybe next time you will chase that lion." He insisted even pointing to the bushes outside the building.

"Ok," Paul replied.

"Then this little guy turned toward the chaos that was almost upon us, waved his hand, and spoke. It was beautiful." John made a motion with his good hand replicating what he saw. "The wind became violent, the rain and lightning were blinding, confusing my enemies. Just like he owned it all, had all the authority that God gave."

"Then what?" Paul asked.

"The mountain behind us." John laughed. "We just walked up the mountain, maybe a bullet or two struck the ground close. I was busted up pretty bad."

"Did you know him before that day?"

"No, not a clue who this guy was," John said, shrugging his shoulders. "As we reached the top of that mountain, we turned to face the violent storm he had brought us through in the valley below. I heard men yelling in confusion, I saw gunfire as they even shot their people in the darkness. Small tornadoes sent a cloud of dust right through them, they did not know who was friendly. Their dogs attacked each other. What came to destroy me, was turned against itself."

"Did you ever catch this guy's name? Superman possibly?" Paul asked like a kid.

"Yes, Immanuel!" John said proudly.

Paul remembered the cemetery worker. His name was also Immanuel, he thought, but never mentioned it.

John continued, "He took me over and set me upon a rock. That hurt, I think I even hollered a little. He calmly walked over to his donkey that was tied to a bush. Then produced bread and wine. I was in a panic because during the mass exodus in the valley, I lost my rifle, pistol, tomahawk, everything that I valued. I felt so naked. And this little Hispanic man was concerned about me taking some religious ceremony."

"I am sure you were hungry after that," Paul added thinking his breakfast was wearing off.

John nudged Paul. "It was why Immanuel was doing this." John coughed into his hand. "Immanuel said that Papa wanted to talk to me as he dug through the saddlebags on his donkey. The chaos in the valley silenced." John examined my reaction. "All I wanted was my rifle," John said. "Immanuel said, where I was going next, old ways would not work anymore." John shrugged his shoulder. "Next, the little guy placed the bread in my hand, and we ate it together. He said it was for the broken parts that can now be healed. We then drank the wine, for blood that was spilled. It was beautiful," John said.

Paul listened intently. "So, you were hired to kill someone, then betrayed by Lycan, shot to pieces, and a little Hispanic man named Immanuel picked you up and carried you to a safe place. Then he offered you bread and wine because Papa wanted to talk with you?" Paul asked.

"Yes, it sounds rather crazy, but meanwhile, I asked if Immanuel had any medicine for my wounds, and he denied any healing agents. He said Papa was more concerned about my heart and soul than my fleshly wounds that would heal on their own."

Paul had enough of this, as it stirred anger within him. "Who is Papa?"

"I am taking you there, slowly. Just be patient." John urged Paul to listen and to sit back down. "But first I had to come back home to America, for a new beginning. The only address I knew was a small farm in Louisiana, where my Mamaw lived. I was a child when I visited there but life took me far, far away. The only home I knew, that I enjoyed and remember being loved. The farm is where my life changed."

CHAPTER 4

"**J**ohn Hunt," my Mamaw yelled out, "your Mamaw needs your help, baby. Don't be wasting this glorious Saturday."

I was sleeping well. If her shout was not enough to get someone out of bed, though, the smell of her buttermilk biscuits and coffee was. I groaned and raised myself out of bed.

I was only thirty years old, but I was weighed down by a life of shame and regret. The wounds of my last encounters with death had almost healed, but my right shoulder hurt when I completed the morning chores, and my left thigh was still pretty stiff. I rubbed the soreness as I stood by my bed, but cold muscles tended to hold in pain. My back hurt just a little. I didn't remember why. Maybe I fell while bullets snapped twigs and air all around me.

My Mamaw could pick up on anything that was out of order. I dare anyone to stand in front of her and say everything is okay. She could know your thoughts with just a look. Mamaw never used her discernment as a source of power over anybody. I learned this quickly after I arrived from Mexico.

The smell of breakfast made its way to my room, so I quickened my routine, driven by hunger. But as I stood up, my healing wounds protested. Before I put my shirt on, I took a close look at my shoulder, admiring the gaping hole left and thankful that no bone was broken when that bullet found its target. I stretched my shoulder slowly and continued. I was glad to wake up on this particular Saturday morning because I had the same dream I've had several times before. The vision of finding my younger self alone under a tree. An uncertain feeling rushed over me.

I opened the door and left my upstairs room. As I walked along the hall to the stairs, I admired the puzzles framed along the walls. The Last Supper. For some reason, I looked a little harder at that puzzle, hoping I might find myself somewhere hidden in the frame. I'm sure I fit in somewhere important with thirteen people in a picture. I looked at these puzzles every morning for almost a month, and the mysteries still caught my attention long enough for a quick glance.

I walked down the stairs, and before I even reached the bottom, I could hear the oven vent blowing, so I knew bacon or sausage would be in my future.

My Mamaw's house had the most inviting smells I have ever experienced. With fresh-baked bread and homemade wine sitting on the table every day, who wouldn't feel at home? Her house was a comfortable place to live in, even in Louisiana's hot and humid summers. She lived just about twenty miles south of Shreveport, and the Red River to her east made for a perfectly secluded little farm.

I stopped just before taking my seat at the dining room table and admired the M1 Garand over the living room fireplace. The spare clip of ammunition collected dust beside it. Mamaw burned a fire almost all year round. Only when it was hot did she subside.

The china cabinet to my left had a collection of her favorite dishes, only used during special occasions. The oversized kitchen doors were to my right. As I limped slightly to the dining table for breakfast, my Mamaw gave me a kiss on the cheek.

"Morning, sugar, it's a delight to see you," she said, I smiled and kissed her back. "Baby, you're walking better every day, and I'm glad to see you smiling a bit more."

"You should have seen the other guy," I said playfully.

"Don't joke, John Hunt. I was ready to grab my shotgun when you showed up here the way you did."

I shrugged my shoulders, but she kept her eyes on me as I leaned on a chair for stability, and smiled.

"You had that dream again, didn't you?" she asked. I sipped my coffee, not meeting her eyes. "You ready to talk about it yet?"

I sighed and patted the chair next to mine. Eagerly, Mamaw sat.

"I was walking through a field and noticed a tree—a beautiful tree. I approached the tree to get closer and saw a young boy upset. It was only as I got right in front of him that I realized the little boy was me."

"Sugar that says something. A young man trying to find himself. You push towards finding those answers to that dream, and your life's struggles will unfold. And you will find what your soul longs for; dreams are the doors to our very souls." As she turned back toward the kitchen, she stopped and said quickly, "I would look into how you felt about your father abandoning you." I flinched, spilling my coffee on my lap.

"Dang, woman," I mumbled from the dining table as Mamaw was having a second conversation behind those kitchen doors.

Mamaw had a friend she called Papa that she talked and prayed to from the other side of those kitchen doors. I was not allowed to cross through the threshold. She said it was a part of a plan for me to be patient. And at the right time, this process would all make sense. I did peek a time or two but was chastised by her instead. I do not think she realized how dangerous I could be.

"Find yourself," Mamaw said from her kitchen. Like a February rain, a cold chill ran down my back, my heart began to ache, and the dark cloud that would come and go in my life suddenly appeared. There it was again, that monster in me; I had to watch my words, attitude, and motives. As the pain swelled in my heart, Mamaw came behind me, kissed my head, and said, "John, you are such a blessing to me." Her words could soothe my attitude when my father, her son's, name was mentioned. "Smile, baby," she said. I just gave a slight grin, hiding my hurt. Slowly, the pain went away.

My Mamaw brought some honey to put on the table, and I was like a kid at Christmas, "Sausage is on its way," she said.

"I hope the next woman in my life can do half the stuff you do," I said.

"Well, John, the beginning of something comes from nothing, so just declare it out loud to get the ball moving," she replied with an arrogant laugh. I took another sip of coffee.

"No woman could tolerate me," I mumbled.

"See, John Hunt, out of the mouth the heart speaks," she said from behind those kitchen doors. "There is a pain to change and also the pain of staying the same."

My Mamaw had gray hair that went just below her ears and eyes that could look right through you when it was time to listen. She was a beautiful woman at seventy-five years of age, and her work ethic was something I have yet to see anyone duplicate. We had some good conversations between those kitchen doors, and I was entertained by the activity I couldn't see from this side. I have heard pies fall to the floor and numerous jars of jam splatter against that tile, followed by, "Nothing like a good mess for Papa and me to clean up." Just sitting at that table, and listening to her gave me some joy. Well, that and those buttermilk biscuits and coffee.

"Holy crap," I yelled as I jumped straight out of my chair.

"Baby, you okay?" My Mamaw said from behind those kitchen doors.

"That cat of yours just brushed up against my leg. I liked to have wet myself." I yelled. My Mamaw's laugh carried through the door.

"Now, John, just push him away if he bothers you. He does not mean any harm," she said. I thumped that cat on the nose, and he bolted upstairs. "John, don't be mean to my cat. He's just saying good morning," she said.

I didn't answer because my anxiety was straight through the roof, and I was trying to calm myself down. So I began to remember why I came here, and I took big deep breaths of air. My face was warm, and I knew my blood pressure had spiked.

"This is nonsense. I'm thirty years old with blood pressure issues," I shouted, and I tried to savor my morning. I tried to enjoy this fantastic breakfast, just thinking about my next move in life, and for the first time, I didn't have any plans. I was getting nervous again because, without a vision, a man can wander through life without reason, and become a samurai without a master. Over the last few weeks, my mind was beginning to drift, casting all my problems and failures into a whirlwind. My life for years consisted of gunshots and having to look over my shoulder regularly, always sitting with my back against the wall, but here I had no schedule or real reason to be on guard.

My Mamaw's Cur dog began to bark at me through the glass window of the backdoor, and I spun around expecting a fight, my heart beating quickly. The dog was licking the sliding glass door, hoping for a handout from the dinner table. I became calmer in more hostile situations, but here, I had an uneasy feeling that would give me stomach pains as I had no clue what life had in store for me, and I had no understanding of a life without violence. At times this place could be like the house of freaking horrors—a cat randomly touching you, animals outside always making noise—and my blood pressure would rise.

"Be anxious for nothing, baby. That's what Papa always tells me," she said from behind that kitchen door.

All I knew was I had gone as far as I could go, and the letter from my Mamaw had given me an excellent chance to start over. I was struggling to find my place in this cruel and unforgiving world. Mentally, I was exhausted, and the monster inside me caused a great deal of depression. Not in seasons, but in persistent feelings of grief. No matter how much money I made or the number of contracts I could have taken, my dreams were still haunted by my victims and my inability to let go.

Ever hear a man beg for his life? I had seen men promise me more money and power before I killed them. Some believed I was cruel in all that I did, but I had standards. No women, no kids, and no innocent blood, which was my code of ethics.

As I sat at her table enjoying the biscuits and coffee, I heard my Mamaw stirring around behind those doors. It sounded like a war of pots and pans, and I laughed from just wondering what went on back there. The kitchen door flew open.

"John, you still have that letter I wrote to you?" she asked.

"No, but I remember the address that was on it," I said.

She just looked out the window and said, "What a beautiful invitation." My Mamaw brought me some sausage and took a seat, looking at me very seriously, and said, "Baby, you have been in here for a couple of weeks now. I think it's time we talk about something".

"I think that's a great idea, lay it on me; I could use a good mission right now. My body is healing," I replied while adding a piece of sausage to my plate. My Mamaw grinned at me, turned around in her chair, and pointed at a picture on the wall.

"I've never noticed that picture before," I said.

My Mamaw giggled and said, "Well, John Hunt, that's the first time you sat in that chair for more than twenty minutes, and look what you found."

I went back to the picture and noticed an old house, maybe a dog trot house or something.

I said quickly, "It's a house," with shrugged shoulders.

Mamaw said, "Baby, if that's all you see, Lord, open his eyes." She laughed loudly, holding her stomach.

"I don't get it."

"Honey, sometimes you have to look at something closely for a long time to fully see the beauty of any situation. There is meaning in that painting. You just haven't found it yet but keep thinking about it, and let me know what you discover."

"Do what?" I scoffed.

"You heard me, John Hunt. Learn to enjoy the things you can't see right away because your eyes can tell a story." I continued to stare at her.

"Now, John Hunt, do as your Mamaw says and learn to be still, and Papa will open your eyes."

"Is this some type of training?" I asked.

My Mamaw got up and went to the kitchen, disappearing through the swinging door. Pots and pans scattered, and I heard her snort. "Stupid men, never appreciate the good details."

So I turned again to the painting on the wall. My Mamaw wanted me to stare at a picture, determine the meaning of it, and learn to be still so Papa could talk to me? I just didn't understand. The kitchen noise ceased as Mamaw came barreling back through the kitchen door, took her seat and pointed the finger at me, and said, "Baby, welcome to your Bootcamp."

"Bootcamp?" I asked.

My Mamaw just grinned. "Yes, honey, this is how Papa trained me, and he wants to train you as well."

"This is ridiculous! You expect me to put my plans in the hands of someone you talk to behind those kitchen doors?" I hate to admit it, but I rolled my eyes in disbelief.

"First of all, John, Papa loves you, and this was his plan," she said.

"To stare at a picture on your wall after breakfast," I said with a smirk.

"No baby, to bring you back home so you can find the peace and rest that you have been searching for. Papa knows your heart, and it is in his nature to be whatever you need Him to be. The picture, John, is just a training tool to open up your mind and to learn to be still and not be anxious when you do not have the answers you want right now."

I was beginning to see that my old ways of doing things would not work in this place. What I held so close and valued for security was absolutely useless.

"John, will your gear help you here? Can your gun and equipment bring you security, a security that will only lead to death and betrayal?"

"Did you say betrayal?" I sat up in my seat. "My gear was scattered in the desert of Mexico."

"Papa is your only security now. Surrender your control of the now to Papa, who is your future," she said.

"So what about the betrayal part of this conversation?" I reminded her.

My Mamaw just shrugged her shoulders. "We aren't going to talk about betrayal yet, baby. One issue at a time. Papa and I have to get you calmed down first. You can't light a candle in a hurricane John."

I did not want to go back and hunt men. I was desperate for a new beginning. I turned my chair to face her directly, giving this a fair try.

"John, what do you want for yourself right now?" she asked.

"I don't want to go back to my old life!" I said quickly.

"So, what are you going to do about that, John Hunt?" she whispered. For about the fourth time that morning, I just stared at my beloved Mamaw for what seemed to be an eternity, and somehow ray of sunlight seemed to find its way into our conversation.

My Mamaw, while taking a sip of her coffee, reminded me, "Country living is not so bad, always something to tend to." The Cur dog was whining at me through the glass door, and his nose was pushed against the door, leaving a wet smudge.

"All eyes on me," I said, as he wagged his tail against the concrete floor of the back porch.

My Mamaw began to get comfortable in her chair, and I watched a glow begin to surround her as if she could have been an angel. She had her hands raised and was singing. And something rested upon Mamaw like the sunlight through a clean window. I was astonished by her disposition. A cool breeze blew through the room, causing the curtains to move back and forth. The breeze seemed to be searching for a place to rest.

"What was that?" I said as the hairs on my arm were standing straight up.

"Well, that is just Papa showing out like he does. Give him an inch, and he takes a mile." She laughed. She then paused and said, "Honey, what is on your mind? And take your time. Nobody rushes anybody here."

"Uh, well, so what you're saying is that not knowing is still believing and trusting in my old ways of doing things will no longer work for me in this place?"

She sat right up in her chair and said, "Bingo, honey, now you're thinking right because the old things are passing away, and the new things are upon you. Learn to be still, John, and peace will find you."

"We are going to come back to betrayal. It's what got me here in the first place," I said as the one who betrayed me in Mexico was on my mind.

"Enjoy this time of training baby. Rome was not built in a day, so you will have to practice this new stuff for a while, but Papa is going to help you!" she said, clapping softly.

She stopped right before she walked out the front door.

"John, your training begins when you choose to take the picture and find out its meaning. Papa never forces himself on anyone because he is love, and love always allows other choices. No matter what, sugar, your Mamaw will love you the same." She disappeared out the house's front door, and her house cat followed her. Today was not an ordinary conversation for her and me, but my Mamaw knew I was ready for something new. I was about to be humbled.

I knew our lesson was over for today, but I needed a nap to process what had just happened. I could see a glimmer of hope, which began to ease my anxiety. As I rested on what that picture could mean, the name Papa seemed to echo inside me, trying to open up a realm not of logic but of curiosity.

I sat there in the chair, tapping my fork against the table, hesitating. Standing up and taking the painting would start a new journey and acknowledge that this Papa character is real. I could have easily moved on and enjoyed my life of being unaccountable, selfishly pursuing the next dollar bill. Instead, I was being tutored by my Mamaw on the things of this mysterious God.

My anxiety had decreased to just a few butterflies in my stomach. I could control some aspects of this, but not much. That old grandfather clock chimed as I pushed my chair back and took the painting off the wall. It was the right time to take this journey more seriously.

CHAPTER 5

I took the painting off the wall because I could feel a hint of direction for the first time in a long time; I had to trust that the move was more significant than the direction my life was headed. I held on to the painting as if it were the holy grail or the secret ingredient in McDonald's French fries.

My Mamaw's cat stuck his head out of the laundry room and stared at me. He was curious about what I was doing. "Hey, momma's boy!" I told him. That cat walked out quietly and passed me as I returned my focus to the painting. I no sooner turned away fully when that cat bit me on the back of the leg and took off running upstairs. I stomped the floor to scare him, followed by a few swear words and a vow to get even. I rubbed the sore spot while laughing some. The cat had returned to the base of the stairs and was playfully flicking his tail. "There can only be one king in a house," I said jokingly. I gave him an evil stare back and slowly moved forward, stalking him like a lion. That cat froze solid and waited until I was only a few feet away to run up the stairs to hide, waiting for his next chance to attack as I returned to my seat.

The picture was a beautiful painting, with an old country house setting by the river, full of cypress trees and flowers with a beautiful view. The wood on the house appeared very old and began to rot from the southern humidity.

In the south, Louisiana is known for its sweltering, muggy days. A man can sweat just standing outside, so I related to the painting immediately.

Something caught my attention, the house was old, but the windows were big and clean, almost fancy. I did not see one thing in the picture that was worth more than a few thousand dollars; not a big truck or an expensive car. The flowers around the house showed time and attention, neatly pruned and beautifully laid, but nothing expensive to elevate the people forward into more significant possessions. Why would someone put charming features on an old house? The roof was still ok, and the foundation looked stable, but the windows? Why the windows?

I also noticed a massive front door cracked open; the door was something a rich man would desire. Why does the painter emphasize lovely windows and doors but lack attention to the body of the house, highlighting rotten wood and age?

"That is not the American dream," I said quietly. A man wants a nice truck, a home, a woman, and respect.

I heard the front door open, and Mamaw walked back into the house holding the mail; she saw me holding the picture and kept walking.

"By owning nothing, you have everything," she said while dancing back into the kitchen. "This is not the American dream," I shouted. I could hear her behind the doors of her kitchen.

"You can own so much stuff that the stuff you own now owns you. A man only needs one god in his life, John Hunt," she said. I was waiting for her as she stepped out from behind those doors.

"I am almost ready to talk about all I have done in the last seven years, but not yet," I said.

"I know, baby, but an onion has layers. Papa and I are pulling off one layer at a time, and you're talking from a place of insecurity right now. You're gonna get your momentum back."

This woman had a head of wisdom on her, she sees right through me like I have a sign on my forehead. "John, I will never force you to talk about what you have done for the last seven years, but I love you. I still see you with children, and you are better than all the lies you have believed since your childhood."

I had to look away to keep from breaking, "I have done horrible things."

She just smiled and said, "Honey, your eyes have talked to me for the last three weeks, and so has Papa. You are going to be more beautiful than you can ever imagine, and you will find yourself."

I took a deep breath in and let it out.

"So what do I call this place that I am in right now?" I asked. The blessing of owning nothing echoed within me. Now I understood why the house in the painting had old wood of great age and contained extensive beautiful features inside and out. The windows and doors could be ways of seeing in and outside an individual, his perspectives, and his persona. The flowers were the blooming seasons that illuminated the true identity of that old house. The question remained, was the house a person or an object? The blessing of owning nothing again whispered to my heart.

"This season will be painful," she said, but her smile was encouraging.

I had begun my journey into the realm of the unknown, a place of no boundaries. Still, at the same time, significant limitations were present. I could not analyze much, but I began to feel my heart open just a little. How deep did this rabbit hole go? Well, I would have to say as deep as my mind and spirit were willing.

My Mamaw owned about three hundred acres off the Red River; what some people call river-bottom land that is flat—a perfect place for a cowboy. As I walked back into the living room to decide what my day might look like, my Mamaw gave me a brilliant idea.

"John, what about you taking a little adventure out past my south fence? There has always been a good place to hunt wild pigs. I could use that meat to make good sausage."

"And what gun do you have that I can borrow?" All of mine were scattered in that valley in Mexico, a long way from there.

"Take that old thing above the fireplace," she responded and gave me wandering eyes.

I had been eyeing that rifle the first day I arrived.

"Yeah, that is correct, baby," she said before disappearing into her kitchen.

I picked up the rifle from the gun rack just over the fireplace. M1 Garand Springfield Armory. The barrel looked good, and the action needed to be wiped and oiled. The clips were already loaded, so I put one in the gun, slamming the bolt shut, and another in my back pocket.

"How do you like it?" she asked as she wiped her hands dry on a towel.

"I really like it. I always wanted one."

"Here is a knife to put in your belt loop; it was your Grandfather's." She smiled. "We can talk about the rifle later; I will be thinking about a price."

"Please do," I said, hopeful.

"John Hunt, we do one thing at a time around here. First, we talked about resting your anxious mind and not using your old ways. Second, you focus on the meaning of that picture, which we will discuss next, and then we discuss betrayal. People are attracted to peace, baby, not a dog that will snap at them unexpectedly."

"Okay," I said, not wanting to accept my stillness and maybe fidgeting a little, almost wanting to express some negativity.

"John Hunt, while you're learning to trust in Papa, don't you think serving other people will help pull a layer off that onion?" my Mamaw asked.

"I reckon it would—not really sure of all of this God stuff," I mentioned. The monster growled within me selfishly. "You mean like rake somebody's yard?"

"John, learning to serve is almost like opening a window and letting a cool breeze blow through the house," she said with a smile.

I just stood there biting my lip, a habit I developed in childhood. "So, when Papa or whatever it was that blew through your dining room? Who served so that could happen?" I asked.

"Keep thinking like that, and Papa is gonna blow your mind."

I nodded to show I understood but kept my emotions and expectations down. Any momentum would have to be met on a mutual understanding.

The M1 felt bulky. It was heavier than what I was used to. The thought of walking out into the unknown to hunt something felt familiar, but this time I was not chasing a man. A cold nose touched my hand.

"So, brother, you want to tag along?"

That Cur dog was eager and ready to work, so we both stood silently. I gazed out into my new backyard. The manure smelled ripe, but a breeze brought in the fresh smell of honeysuckle from a nearby vine. My past still called to me, but I ignored the feelings. There was something else trying to take over. I could feel a shift within the depths of me. Ever since that breeze blew through the house that morning, I had been a little calmer, even if it had only been an hour ago.

I stepped off the concrete patio covered with porch chairs and hummingbird feeders. Wasps were flying overhead, looking for moisture. Her backyard was fenced in. Full of flowers and loaded with green grass with a small garden in the corner. Her labor outside and inside her house was evidence of my Mamaw's hardworking character. My Mamaw's backyard was incredible. Everything had a place and order, from the bird feeders to the rose bushes.

I reached the first fence separating the backyard from the livestock she had pastured. I grabbed the latch holding the gate together, and the gate almost fell off the hinges. I caught it right as it fell. The Cur dog scooted beside me, almost anticipating the gate falling.

"Man, I need to fix this," I said. The barn animals began to talk, almost laughing at the scene. The Cur dog looked back one time towards the house, making sure Mamaw did not have another job for him to do. I closed the last fence, and a cow mooed, thinking somehow food might be given out. The Cur and I walked maybe a hundred yards toward the unknown. I took a knee, feeling out the terrain as a flock of geese flew over, heading south. I grabbed a handful of dirt, smelling it before rubbing it onto my hands—just tradition.

The Cur dog was eager, and I watched him throw his nose up in the air, trotting off in front of me. The Cur and I managed to find a game trail as we walked through the tall grass that had game trails from a squirrel to a deer.

The wilderness is a great place to think. By casting down sorrows and picking up, adventure can set the soul on fire.

We passed a fresh mud puddle that was disturbed, and I could see the hog tracks in and around the water. I followed the tracks and watched the Cur dog's walk become a trot. His tail was sticking up, and his ears bent forward to enhance his hearing. A blue jay called in distress.

"Well, now everyone knows we are here," I said, placing my iron sights on that bird. "Yeah, I could dust you real good." I thought.

We had tall grass on all sides, but several tall oak trees stood out like our long-lost friends. I used those mighty oaks as markers just in case I got lost. I knew at dark the cows and chickens would give their last call, but that was eight hours away. The wind was blowing in my face and took my scent far away. The tracks we followed had disappeared, but so had my sidekick. If he wasn't with me, maybe he knew something that I do not. I continued my stalk quietly, easing my feet to the ground, step by step and listening for a dog to bark, signaling he had caught something.

I was now a thousand yards away from home, quickly seeing the Red River. I took a knee and was thankful. Not many people have a view like this in their backyard. Some have to pay lots of money to pack a rifle and walk into the unknown, looking for something. I heard a group of ducks quack on a nearby oxbow, letting everyone know of their contentment, not stressed or worried about tomorrow. I stopped, looked down at my feet and saw a fresh hog track, boosting my momentum back into the hunt. I found a tree with new mud smeared about knee-high.

"Wow, that is a giant hog," I said, checking the soil with my finger.

Suddenly, I heard that Cur bark, and I kneeled down immediately to get a direction. I closed my eyes, listening; the dog's bark got quieter and louder simultaneously, making it difficult to pinpoint. I moved forward and found myself turning to the west, making an abrupt right turn into the grass as tall as me and more like a jungle of vegetation. I had to use my gun and push the grass down before me, making a path. The Cur dog was now more than 100 yards in front of me, and I could see a group of willow trees up ahead shaking violently. I began to hear the hog squealing. My adrenaline shot straight up, my focus and confidence rose quickly, and my heart began to beat faster. So did my intentions.

I could gain several yards at a time by lunging forward and pushing the grass down. The grass left its mark on my face and arms. The squeal was deafening now, and that Cur was barking, but I could not see that dog for the tall grass. He was right in front of me, not 30 feet away, and I could not see anything but the trees shaking from the fight. I had just a few feet to go. It just seemed like a wall there with no end. I pushed the tall grass one last time and fell face-first into an open space the size of a small room.

This fight between dog and hog had gone on for so long that the grass was no longer standing. The only thing left standing was that small group of willow trees on the right corner of this death ring. My presence was unnoticed until I stood up from my fall. I was not welcomed into this fight by any means, but I noticed the hog was bleeding from his right ear, and the Cur had some blood on his right shoulder. I quickly scanned the death circle of smashed-down debris, knowing that the tall grass would be my hiding place if I had to retreat. That Cur was circling the hog, barking the whole time.

"I am here, brother," I yelled. The dog had one job—to keep the hog circling, allowing his master to take the shot. The monster in me instinctively reached for my tomahawk, but I did not bring it with me.

The hog turned to face me as blood dripped from his head. All I could see were those eyes and teeth at first, and everything about this hog was all business. The hog was jet black with a Mohawk down the middle of his back, and angry does not begin to describe him. His attitude was somewhere between hatred and malice; the Cur was still circling the hog left to right, taunting that hog while doing his job. The hog was trying to decide whether to charge me or keep fighting that Cur. He constantly moved toward me and then turned to face that black-mouthed cur. Both were quick, and the hog weighed twice as much as my eighty-pound companion.

The pig ran at me, but that Cur dog jumped on his back, spinning him back around away from me.

I raised my rifle while that Cur kept that hog spinning around in a circle. I placed my sights behind the pig's ear and squeezed the trigger at twenty feet. Dust, fur, and blood filled the air, and that hog fell to the ground like a sack of potatoes. The Cur walked over to the side of that death ring and laid down, out of breath, panting for air. I kneeled beside him under a willow tree to rest and checked his shoulder. The blood smear did not belong to him.

"My brother, you did great. Thank you for keeping that hog off of me," I grinned. That Cur was still lying on his side, panting for air; I knew we would be there for a minute or two.

I leaned back against that willow tree, pulled a cigar out of my front pocket, and lit the end with my lighter. I did this after every kill, just something I began as a ritual to celebrate a kill or victory. The uninitiated would not understand or recognize the significance of my tradition; it is no different from a lion roaring after a fight, celebrating the moment.

This ground was ours, and we took it from a beast.

"Do you have a name, brother?" I asked while I checked for a snake on the ground before taking my seat. "No? Well, I might have to give you a name," I wiped the sweat from my brow.

That Cur never picked up his head but was lying peacefully and trying to catch his breath. He wagged his tail to acknowledge my request. "Let's see, my friend, you protected me from that pig and guarded my Mamaw's house, so let's call you Santo. It means Saint in Spanish," I said.

That Cur raised his head, then wagged his tail; he sat up, walked over to where I was sitting, and put his head in my lap.

"Next time, try to find something a little bigger. This hog is only twice your size," I said with a laugh. I knew the name was a perfect fit for him and that Cur was like all men who search for a new name and a purpose.

After a while, I stood up, slung the rifle behind my back, finishing my cigar. That Cur dog just leaned against my leg and licked me. The dog owned nothing but had everything.

CHAPTER 6

"**M**an, I am out of shape," I said struggling to get a full breath as I carried the pig on my shoulders. The blood from the animal was starting to run down my shirt. It was warm but nevertheless, I could buy a new one tomorrow. The weight of the hog on my shoulders was enough to remind me that the double portions of food at my Mamaw's dinner table had not been helpful but I enjoyed it deeply.

"Santo the hog hunter," I said, as he marked his territory. I was amazed at how well Santo worked that day with little training before my arrival.

My companion was solid in battle and I knew he was reliable above all others, but it was entertaining to see him interrogate the grasshoppers and other bugs on the way back home, sniffing and nipping at them playfully. My new friend was curious about everything on the trail, but he never left my side. I was struggling with the pig's weight that was bearing down on my back and shoulders, stretching my lungs to the fullest and reminding me that I was still a mortal.

"Santo, I think I need to lay off second helpings from Mamaw!" I said while taking a deep breath of air and fumbling with my rifle in the tall grass surrounding me. The game trail I was following home was no wider than myself.

This place had to be tempting to all the foxes and coyotes that ran wild out there. Every ten steps produced another game trail of some type, typically much smaller than the one I was following home. I saw mostly rabbit trails in the low grass; there was no telling what really had been there.

Santo caught the scent of something and darted off to the right with his tail straight up in the air.

"Santo no."

I called off the chase to the unknown for another time, as my back and shoulders had had enough for the day. Santo was almost in grass taller than himself but returned to his rank beside me still seeking and searching for another adventure hoping for another shot at a beast in a thicket. The dog heeled on my left side, walking back in sync but began to whine. The warrior in some does not die, it just regroups and moves on looking for round number two and ignoring all the signs of weakness and age.

Something caught my attention where the grass was pushed down flat in a few places, I saw several really big hog tracks going into a dark thicket. I stopped for a moment and thought to myself, that's where I would be. I looked back at the tracks and Santo sniffed with excitement at the fresh prints.

"Man, these are only a few hours old at the most. Yeah, that's a monster alright." I said.

Santo put his head down and looked in the direction the tracks were going with his ears laid back. He wanted another fight, but I was exhausted and the tracks had to come from a pig easily three hundred pounds, maybe a shade under. Santo whined.

"Brother, I am not saying we can't catch that pig, but just not to-day." I turned without saying anything else, hoping that black-mouthed Cur would follow because at this point my nine-pound M1 was becoming a burden. Santo caught up to me several minutes later.

At the gate, Mamaw was holding something in her hand as she leaned up against that fence.

"Maybe she is holding a shot of adrenaline, but I would settle for a glass of water," I said, hoping to catch my breath sometime soon. I could see her smiling from there through the sweat pouring from my forehead; she was pleased with our actions. Santo began to whimper with his tail and head raised high.

"Well, brother, thank you for getting me back home."

I could see Mamaw up ahead as I walked tiredly toward her. The sun and clouds are waging a war on who could cover my Mamaw the best, and the sun was always the champion. Light just seemed to follow her as if something from above had ordered the heavens to watch over her. That woman was proud of me. I waved the rifle in the air to signal that I saw her. But I did know that one day she would find out who I really was and I wondered if she would still love me.

"I have somebody in mind that we can give some of the meat to John. I just needed some sausage and this person could use some help," she said. "Sometimes, John, we have to take a walk about in the wilderness just to get a revelation."

I could see she had her watering pail ready and sitting beside her on the ground.

"Those flowers are calling my name baby; even the plants need to be refreshed," she said. "I had to take care of you first. You are more valuable than these plants," she said with a big possum grin. "Well, I do like my plants," she said while looking back at me and pinching me on the arm.

I had walked through the gate holding that prize and Mamaw kept saying, "My baby learning to serve while he waits on Papa."

I reached out to get that glass of water.

"Just peeling off a layer of that onion," I said while tossing the dead hog to the ground. Mamaw's slaughter pig a few yards away went crazy running around in his pen and squealing to high heavens, knocking over his food bucket and banging into his pen.

"It's not your time yet, so settle down!" Mamaw told the wide-eyed pig. Not only was the pig spooked by death, but the chickens were spooked and began to run around the yard and lost a few feathers.

"My god, you bring one dead animal in this yard and everything goes crazy," I mentioned.

"That's right sugar when something dies, it disturbs everything around it. I never fully understood how men could kill each other so easily," she said while shaking her head. "Death kills more than just a smile, John Hunt; death also kills the soul."

I could feel my guard go up for a second, thinking Mamaw was going to ask me a personal question, she didn't have a filter on her mouth.

I could still feel that uncomfortable distance that lingers between individuals while trying to establish an order of power. Death is something I have seen plenty of and I was surprised how all the animals reacted to seeing something lifeless tossed to the ground in front of their eyes.

"John, go and take a seat on our porch and rest before you get this hog cut up, please unload that gun," she commanded I eased over to my resting place, my back was tight and my legs were on fire but I took a seat on that porch chair and laid my rifle on the table close to me, always near.

"Is there any way the people down the road who need the meat cannot just come pick it up? I don't mind tossing that pig in the back of their truck," I said before taking a big gulp of ice water. Santo was busy checking everything out inside the fence making sure he could still call this place home.

"Well, sugar, that is not a bad idea but since it is a single mom with three kids to feed, I think you can cut it up and package the meat for her. We have all the tools here to cut, process, and package that pig for the family. Do you think she can do all that by herself without her spending a good deal of money?"

Mamaw gave me the usual stare that I had felt the last several weeks, so I nodded my head in agreement with my Mamaw and I asked how she wanted the meat butchered.

"Sausage, pork chops, and roast," she said with a big ole grin.

"I named your dog 'Santo'," I said, changing the subject.

Mamaw turned to acknowledge my words and let me finish.

"That Cur dog is a great protector and pretty salty on his feet when salvation is what a man needs. It was fixing to get bad out there if Santo had not been there to keep that hog off of me."

Mamaw had turned to go inside her house, so I relaxed completely and was fixing to close my eyes. It was just so peaceful out there, nobody rushed anybody. The most stressful thing out there was to put gravy or ketchup on your food. I laughed to myself on that issue, but still, I was uneasy most of the time. I had not surrendered as I needed to the atmosphere of that place, but I was trying.

When the backdoor opened, Mamaw presented me with a skinning knife and a sharpening stone. If she knew what all I had done with a knife she might not be so eager to hand me a blade.

"Honey, before you get started on cutting up that pig, let me ask you a question," she spoke as I was gulping down the last of the ice water.

"I am all ears, Mamaw," I said with water dripping down from my mouth.

"Well, John, you have a choice to make and you are free to choose whatever you want to do. You can stay here with me or you can move on to the next phase of your life. Remember, there are things we have not discussed yet, and take your time answering," she reminded me. I looked out past her south fence and admired all that was around me, the animals moving to-and-fro without the slightest sense of fear.

"My body is healing rather quickly and I seem to be more at peace and happy here. I am stressed, but only because I lack the stillness that I need to function here."

The eyes of Mamaw were fixed on me.

"John, by you staying here, your chances of dealing with your past will greatly increase because the fewer distractions you have—the fewer things are pulling for your attention. What stress do you have here other than the negative emotions that live down in your soul, suppressed by hurt and confusion? Your wounds go deeper than just some years back and you already know this, John."

I tried not to say anything but take in what was being said, it was difficult but I had to listen. I leaned forward and grabbed the skinning knife and the sharpening stone. Once again, she was spot on and there was no hiding some of my weaknesses, something I would never expose to another hired gun. I quietly began to sharpen the knife and I could feel those eyes staring at me, waiting for me to speak. I had no words of knowledge or quick comebacks to take the conversation to a different level. I felt like I was backed into a wall, so I waited for an opening and I began to confess some old feelings that I had never talked about to anyone.

"For the last several years, I had that dream even when I was off doing horrible things," I confessed while not looking directly into her eyes.

"Yes, a boy trying to find himself and such a beautiful invitation," Mamaw cut in, all excited. "Hold it right there, baby, I know there is something else you have not told me in your younger days that keeps reoccurring, a vision or a thought possibly. Papa has already shown me but that journey you must take with Papa only. The event occurred when you were younger. It was deeply personal, like that reoccurring dream. Papa wants to discuss this event because it is the deepest wound of your life, way before you left going off to war. Do you know what the wound is, John Hunt?"

I just stared at the grass at the end of the porch, hoping time would pass and Mamaw would disappear back inside and into that glorious kitchen that I had not been allowed to enter. As despair appeared to wrap its ugly arms around me, Mamaw leaned in really very close.

"Papa was there," she whispered.

"I know where this is going and I am not very excited about this conversation." The breeze outside picked up and the trees began to sway as lightning flashed over the horizon, but Mamaw never acknowledged that Papa was near. The wind was not speaking but I thought I heard a lion roar in the distance. I dismissed it for thunder calling me out from my hiding place.

That alone feeling was beginning to move within me again. I believed it was gone because our earlier conversation over a coffee and biscuit made it disappear. All I could think about was butterflies on me and around me. Why was I thinking about butterflies? When I think about my father, I always think about black butterflies, but I had never spoken about this to anyone. The man within was fading and a lost and broken boy began to speak.

"South America has some of the most beautiful butterflies. There is a black one that will take your breath away," I said, as insecurity covered my whole identity. I shook my head in disbelief at myself and what I had just spoken. This giant of a man was talking in riddles and gibberish, stumbling through logic and his beloved Mamaw could see right through it.

"Does your dream from last night seem clearer now? A man finding a boy hiding by a tree? Are you searching for something, John Hunt? Maybe your younger self?" she asked. I was speechless, but not angry. Mamaw whispered, "John, nothing makes us lonelier than our secrets."

How could she know? Who could have told her?

"John, Papa was there and only he can discuss his heart with you and why that had to happen," she said. I remained silent in that porch chair while Mamaw was giving me time to answer. It was true, nobody there forced anybody to do anything. "Searching for something?" she asked.

For me to acknowledge that Mamaw was right, that I was searching for answers would prove that deep down inside I was still just a wounded little boy hiding from joy and peace. All the things a man owned, including his status in this world, in a moment seemed worthless.

Mamaw walked over to the edge of the porch and picked up her watering pail and began to water her flowers, talking the whole way to her plants.

"That's right my babies, when you're thirsty for life, here is a drink," she just kept saying, while watering all her pots on that porch. I was distracted for the moment and I lost my thought process; while listening to her words.

"Does Papa give you words like that to say?" I asked. Mamaw just winked at me.

"What do you think, that's the most important question?" The mystery I felt at the farm is not found in a book, but experienced. I was at the point where I believed Mamaw looked through a different set of eyes.

"So, in the dream, what does the tree represent, the object that my younger self is hiding beside?" I asked.

"John Hunt, this is a conversation that Papa wants to have with you, so you can discover together," she stated. I was hoping she would give a little more insight, but she was not going to let go of any information about my dream.

"Well, what about just something to chew on until Papa shows up?"

Mamaw was unfazed by my begging for answers but this time she stared at me and she could pick up on my eagerness to find the truth.

"Okay, John Hunt, you want to really know?" she asked. "Where is your father, mother, or wife?" she reminded me.

"That's not fair!" I said with my voice raised as the monster in me came alive. I stood up and grabbed that M1, pulled the bolt back to load it, and walked to the edge of the porch looking for my next war.

"That pig can lay there and rot, I don't care!" I yelled putting a few more rounds into his head, blowing off its lower jaw. My heart was racing, my mind was spinning and the top of my head was hot.

"John Hunt, you almost made your Mamaw pee on herself! Wait, I may have to go check my underwear." Once again, she disappeared into the house, sliding back the sliding glass door. I got a pretty good slap on the arm for that one.

All the animals were running around scared out of their minds. The horse went running to the back of the land, and the cattle began to call to one another, seeking the safety of the herd. The backdoor opened and Mamaw reappeared to continue the conversation.

"Honey, some things you cannot run away from like you have all of your life," she said. "Now do you see why this conversation is for Papa, and not for me?" she asked.

I remained standing on the edge of her porch, lost in thought.

"John Hunt, you are capable of deep, meaningful relationships, despite what your past looks like," she spoke, putting her hands around my waist to establish love.

"I want to talk about betrayal," I said, with no smile on my face. When I looked at her, I sighed, "But, I am willing to talk about the painting first."

"To speak about betrayal now could kill you. Your heart is not ready to talk about betrayal yet baby," she said, as my stomach began to hurt again and I felt pressure around my throat and chest. "John, the process that Papa is taking with you will challenge and then change your heart to produce life, not to take life."

That monster in me just laughed and like a squeaking door, a flood of negative feelings rushed in quickly and I could not raise my head because I had been reduced to just a little broken boy. That was all I was on the edge of that porch in the evening dusk, a little broken boy, lost with no direction and confined to a farm.

"John, your deepest wound is due to be dealt with and no matter how far you run in life, this wound will follow you. Do you now see the importance of staying here and dwelling for a while so you can deal with these negative emotions?"

"Look, I just sat down for a glass of water!" We both laughed as I turned to face her. "I think it would be good for me to stay and see this thing through." I had one request if I stayed. "When are you going to let me into that kitchen of yours—Papa is in there." I smiled at my Mamaw and hoped she would let some intel out.

"My kitchen is special to me. I think if you stick around long enough it will all make sense to you".

"So is it like Old Testament stuff? Where God dwelled behind a door?" I asked curiously.

"It is a veil! And…well, Papa was right," was all she said.

We both stood quietly on the porch. I wanted to hear more of the secrets in her kitchen, but she would not tell me more. "It's almost dark

Mamaw and I have to get this pig cut up and iced down; I will salt it good."

"John, we skin the animals beside that old shed over yonder, beside that old Ford. There is a good light overhanging and rope to tie the animals up with so you can process it and the bags of ice you will need are in the freezer. There is a water hose to clean up your area when you are through. You do that baby, and I will be in the kitchen, getting the chicken fried up. I know you like greens and hot water cornbread," she said.

"Oh man, you had me at hot water cornbread," I said as she laughed.

"John, that picture from this morning is the center of our next conversation," she reminded me as I smiled, eager about that talk.

"Santo is invited." My new companion just loved a good head scratch.

"Of course, honey, I am always ready for good company. Let's say three days from now, on this porch over coffee and blueberry muffins. We can discuss that picture and, John, you're gonna find all the answers you are looking for in due time."

I just smiled, "What a beautiful invitation."

"John, you gonna take that gun with you?"

"Don't I always Mamaw?" I said.

"You cannot use your old ways in a new place, baby. You know this but do as you wish. I know you're learning to trust with baby steps, but you're learning," she said.

"Papa's ways are different from mine. I bet his thoughts are different also," I said.

"His thoughts about you are much higher than yours".

I smiled and picked up my shell casings that were on the grass just off of the porch, they were still warm. I tossed them in my hand, I always liked the sound of brass casings in my hands.

"My carpenter is coming by soon to fix that gate and work on a few fences. He is humble. I believe you will like his company." She turned back to go inside.

And just like that, she went her way and I went mine. I grabbed the skinning knives and made my way off the porch and towards that dead hog. "Santo, that woman is trying to kill me, I believe." But he never even picked his head up and just kept laying there, exhausted from the day's adventure. The sun slowly disappeared and I could already tell that I was going to need the light beside the shed because darkness approached rather quickly. I took the rifle off my back and laid it down on a table. I felt vulnerable like never before, naked like a newborn baby. "This place is gonna kill me, Santo," I said with a little anxiety.

Mamaw laughed from the back porch, "That's right John, learn to trust!"

CHAPTER 7

T he morning sun shined brightly into my room as old glory waved with the changing winds. I stood to my feet and stretched; my body was still a little sore from my wounds in Mexico, one on my left thigh and the other on my right shoulder. I fumbled around the room and looked for a shirt. The smell of sausage or coffee did not exist or permeate the atmosphere.

"Something is different about this day," I said softly. Maybe today is cereal Friday, I thought, or Mamaw was not feeling well. It was different in the house—no banging of pans from the kitchen, I did not hear the washer or dryer going, no slamming of a microwave, so odd.

I opened the door to the hallway and walked to the stairway down to the first floor. Still no sign of anyone. "Is the coffee ready?" Was my sense of smell getting weaker? Slowly I walked downstairs only to step on the cat's tail, and we both screamed. I fell back against the railing. I waited as my heartbeat returned to normal and I picked up some lint on the stairs. I would have never guessed that my life would bring me back to a small farm in Louisiana.

I rubbed my eyes and yawned as I stopped at the bottom of the stairs. It seemed I was alone, just the tick of the grandfather clock for companionship. I couldn't even smell bacon.

"Mammaw!" I yelled out and waited, but no reply. My first reaction was she was outside and probably had the new garden area tilled up. I walked to the kitchen doors and stopped, looking to my left out the back glass door. I could see a donkey tied to a post.

"She went and bought another animal to feed," I said aloud and rubbed my eyes, but no response from the other side of these swinging kitchen doors.

"Is the coffee ready?" I pushed the kitchen doors slightly and knocked gently. "Hello," I said and hit harder. "If you want me to come in, make a little noise," I laughed. The sound of pots and pans ushered me quickly into that kitchen with a smile on my face. I will never forget what I saw next—my first encounter with God.

My Mamaw's pies were scattered all over her kitchen floor, and powerful eyes turned toward me.

I froze as he licked his lips before me. My adrenaline shot to an all-time high as a lion turned to face me. His shoulders were broad and muscled, and veins popped out of his chest. His mane was almost black. My legs began to shake as I froze in fear. He was the image of power.

The lion jumped at me to establish himself as sovereign and slapped the floor with his paw and roared so loud my ears rang; the surge of fear I felt drove me out of that kitchen. I slammed into the dining room table knocking over chairs.

"Mamaw!" I yelled. The furniture tackled me, it seemed, as I tried to catch my feet. I ran through the living room and hoped the lion's roar would silence, but the floor shook as the chase began. The stairway was my escape route to my room; my momentum carried me almost past it. I knocked off several pictures that hung on the wall as I ran up the stairway to my weapon that I kept in my room.

I locked my door and grabbed my gun from beside my bed, pulled the bolt back, and loaded a round into the chamber.

"Mamaw, there is a lion in the kitchen!" I yelled as claws came through my bedroom door as I prepared to fire. "Stay in your room," I shouted with no response from her, and then the lion pulled his claws from the door and ran back down the stairs—the house shook as he rubbed the walls of the stairwell.

The sweat ran down my forehead as I slowly, slowly, opened my bedroom door, and my gun steadied. There were deep claw marks on the hallway stairs but the absence of a lion. The only sound was my heartbeat that raced in my chest. There was no noise in the house whatsoever that I could hear. I made my way to the bottom of the stairs; I braced for contact, my weapon's safety was off, and ready to kill anything that stepped in front of my sights.

I cleared the living room to my right and took big breaths of air; I kept my path to the stairway clear. If I had to fight my way back upstairs, I could barricade myself in my room and leave out the window if the beast was too much for me. As I passed the kitchen table, I could see the bite marks on the back door open wide going outside and claw marks on the door frame. I stopped right before the kitchen and listened for any movement. The silence was deafening. I leaned in slowly to glance inside the kitchen with the doors already swung wide open, gun ready.

I turned quickly to enter the kitchen, finger on the trigger.

"Señor, those things are meant to kill," a little Hispanic man said as the barrel of my M1 rammed into his chest.

My eyes widened in shock. I was surprised to realize that it was none other than the man who had rescued me in Mexico after I had been shot.

Immanuel.

I shook my head for a second as if to clear my eyes. But it didn't work. The same man stood before me. How could he have ended up here when I knew him down there?

My questions were interrupted by the remembrance that there was a lion awaiting execution. I ignored the memory of the Immanuel I met in Mexico and focused on the job at hand. After all, logic told me that this couldn't be the same man.

"Did it get you? Are you alright?" I asked, my breathing shallow from the urgency of my quest.

"What do you mean, Señor?"

"The lion! A lion just came through here. Did he hurt you?" I asked, my question more of a demand than anything else.

His only response was a sly smile and he looked away. He stood in the same place as the lion earlier but had gotten some rags to clean up a mess of pie pans and pie filling. He wore a poor man's uniform, a hard worker that accepted cheap wages.

My heart pumped so hard as I scanned the room for a lion. I could feel my pulse almost burst out of my neck.

"The lion was here in this kitchen," I insisted as he leaned against a counter and poured himself a glass of wine.

"Papa went outside. He got hungry," he laughed. I shook my head in disbelief.

"What are you doing here?" I asked with my rifle lowered, giving into the recognition.

"So, you remember me?" he asked.

The hair on the back of my neck stood on end. It really was him? How was it possible?

"Imm...Immanuel..." I stuttered, with great difficulty.

The sly smile shifted into a wide grin. I could barely look him in the eye, realizing that I had to be losing my mind for all of this to be happening.

"Why are you here?" I asked again. I wasn't going to let him get away with silence.

"I am a carpenter. I fix things, my friend," Immanuel insisted. "We stop by here many times."

"Do not play stupid with me." I pointed my finger at his chest. "What is going on?"

"Your heart was not ready when you first moved here. Heaven has looked your way. We are delighted you are here with us," Immanuel said, but not before he locked the kitchen doors open. "These doors will stay open for you, forever."

I took a deep breath, trying to decide which battle I was going to fight. I could choose the riddles of this man who coincidentally ended up at my mamaw's house, or I could go after the tangible form of a lion. The hunt was calling my name.

"There was a lion here. He chased me." I looked out the kitchen window only to see the usual activity outside, nothing more, my rifle still in my hands.

"The lion has come up from the thicket and is ready to judge," Immanuel said. "He is a warrior and not even close to a tame lion. He could have killed, but he sees good in you," Immanuel suggested and stood beside the kitchen window. Santo barked at the gate leading to the back of the land where the lion dwelt. "My Papa has always been unpredictable. So are you," Immanuel said.

I stood in the kitchen, confused about what was going on.

"Papa!" I exclaimed.

Immanuel enjoyed his morning wine. "He has been waiting for this since your birth. Do not waste it, my friend."

"God left me in my youth," I said.

"No, we never left you. We were in the wind, the sunlight on your face, and the black butterfly that gently flew around you as you cried that day," Immanuel said. "John, rejection is so difficult to overcome, and it is time for that conversation to begin soon. He is good, and nothing like you have imagined true," Immanuel said and looked at the scars on both wrists, rubbing them gently. "It's a reminder of Papa's love for his children, including you," Immanuel said. "Papa has gone back outside. He was hungry. He prefers pork," Immanuel smiled.

"Don't you think it is a little early to be drinking wine?" I asked.

"I am the bread, and I am the wine." He smiled and pointed to the back of the property, the dark thicket. "Go chase that lion, my friend. Papa has the answers. I just prepare the soil so the flower can grow," Immanuel said and took a piece of bread and put butter and jam on it. "Do you want some toast?" Immanuel asked and reached out to give me a slice of toast as a rooster crowed outside.

"Somebody had better start talking, or you're going to see the side of me I have been trying to bury," I raised my voice toward Immanuel.

Santo barked outside, and it calmed my aggression towards Immanuel, who politely took his breakfast and walked past me. I was left alone in the kitchen, feeling lost as Immanuel stopped at the backdoor, almost outside.

"Papa is calling to you. There is a whole new life for you out past that fence, my friend, the answers your soul longs for." Immanuel turned to face the outside area.

"Did John pee himself?" I heard my Mamaw ask Immanuel with a bit of chuckle in her voice. I lingered in the kitchen and tried to digest what had just happened. "John, come here and talk to your Mamaw."

I closed my eyes and focused. I held the countertops of that kitchen sink; my rifle now slung over my shoulder.

"Hold on one second," I demanded. "Nope, I did not pee myself," I whispered and checked. After several minutes, I let go of the kitchen countertop.

Mamaw was outside close to the cow pen, checking on a calf she found that morning.

"I sure hope this momma takes her calf. I am too old to be bottle feeding a rejected calf, I will call Maddie. She will be glad to help," she talked out loud as if somebody was listening. Mamaw carried a bottle to feed the calf.

"I wanted to give you and Papa a chance to meet. I saw him jump over that fence there and run back towards the thicket on the backside of my property. You already met my carpenter Immanuel," she said.

"There was a lion in your kitchen!" I said as she smiled and stopped to pull up weeds growing in one of her many flower beds. She still held that bottle in her hands.

"The last time He was here, he tried to fit through my gate, almost tore it down. He needs to lay off the second helpings of whatever he has been eating," she laughed.

"Is this normal activity?" I asked.

Mamaw shook her head, "No, most of the time, it is natural for a momma cow to accept her calf," she said.

Immanuel spoke up for John. "Mamaw, John wants to know if it is normal for Papa to visit in your kitchen," he said.

"Papa will be whatever He needs to be to reach you. The lion is a symbol of God's power and mercy," she said, taking a breath of air. "That's what He told me and the reason you are here now," she added.

"Mamaw, what is going on?" I left Immanuel's side to get answers from her.

"Since now you know what was behind those kitchen doors, what's the use in talking about it here right now? Today we talk about that painting on the wall after breakfast. The answers to betrayal are out there, not in the comfort of this small farm. Take a walk past that gate and see what you find," she said sternly.

I clutched my rifle as Immanuel finished his wine on the porch but stepped down off the concrete slab to stand beside me. "It's a beautiful invitation, my friend, and anything rooted in love can be perfected." Immanuel nudged me forward. "We will drink wine when you return."

The lion roared in the distance like a rumble of thunder.

"Excuse me," I turned to go back inside to get dressed.

"There is a bit of food in the oven," Mamaw said, as I opened the door to prepare for a fight.

I returned upstairs wearing much more suitable attire to help keep the bugs and thorns off of my legs. My pants had gotten a little tighter, and those second helpings had caught up. I grabbed a biscuit and sausage from the microwave and sat on the porch while Mamaw wrestled with a calf and Immanuel took measurements for his project.

"To serve mankind is always a pleasure," Immanuel said. He was focused on measuring his project, but making partial eye contact. The lion roared softly in the distance.

"I am taking a gun to hunt your Papa, and you are not even concerned that I might have a lion's skin rug or a necklace made from his claws?" I sat on the porch as I finished my breakfast and, with a napkin, cleaned my face. Immanuel was slow to answer.

Immanuel held up his hand to stop me, "A lot had to happen just to get you here and it's a time of celebration for us."

That old Cur dog wanted some of my biscuits. I gave the dog my last bit. "You ready for the biggest fight of your life?" I asked him. He barked, of course, as we both stepped off the porch. Immanuel smiled as we passed him, and he shut the gate behind us.

I sensed the eyes of a lion were already on me. I found a fresh paw print in the mud. It was big, just about a hundred yards from the farm. I began my stalk from there, slowly hunting for something that could pursue me. Careful not to snap any twig or a dry leaf, I made my world much smaller in my mind. The wind would pick up, and I would pause. I listened. Santo bolted, running into a nearby bush, and flushed a few quail.

I motioned to call him back but hesitated, just a faint whistle to maybe stop him with a failed attempt. My sidekick disappeared into the tall grass; perhaps the lion would not eat him. I let the wind pick up just a little before I started to track, looked down at the ground, and almost stepped on a snake. "Wow," I said quietly; it was a water moccasin. "One bite from you, and I would be in a bad spot." I killed it with the butt of my rifle.

I remember what the grass felt like as it rubbed across my body. With the fresh claw marks on random trees, I could feel the lion's power. My eyes became fixed on what was in front of me as I began to find tiny traces of bones—animals that Papa found delightful. The paw prints of a beast pointed me to the thicket up ahead, about fifty yards. The thicket shook as the lion scurried inside the mess of dark brush and grass. I took the safety off of my rifle, ready for a fight, and cautiously moved through the tall grass that was now waist-high. I could feel my heartbeat like a drum in my chest as tunnel vision set in.

I was only fifty yards now from the thicket as the smell of something dead was close. I stopped as the wind changed. The lion showed himself suddenly and I raised my rifle to fire a shot. The lion roared and disappeared back into the darkness; the beast was angry. I had been smelt;

busted as a hunter would say. The lion snapped twigs and broke branches as he moved inside his place of refuge. His grunts of war sent chills up and down my spine as the limbs broke. The beast had found refuge to my left and laid down somewhere for an ambush. The shadows inside the thicket became still. I needed a clear shot but had yet to get one.

I began to circle the lion's thicket. As I stepped on old bones of deer and pig, flies arose from the ground. The smell was strong of death. Again, the limbs and briars shook as the lion ran to find a better position; our eyes meet in the darkness of his dwelling place. I raised my rifle, and he disappeared again.

"I got you now." Slowly, I stalked. Every footstep was precise and calculated amongst the smell of death and bone. Suddenly to my left, those eyes appeared.

The bushes parted, and the lion had come for me. Jaws grabbed the end of the barrel of my rifle. He tried to pull me into his thicket as briars cut my face. His strength was too great, and I was being manipulated, shaken like a leaf. I fired my rifle, and the beast let go. The lion raged forward, knocked me to the ground, and ripped the gun from my hands. The gun soared behind him.

I took some steps back and put distance between myself and the lion. I reached for my knife as the lion circled me, a false charge, a swipe of the mighty paw.

He growled and roared. I had lost sight of my rifle in the tall grass. "I am going to get you and put you in front of that fireplace," I said.

The lion charged me, a claw slashed my forearm, and down to the ground, I went. The lion slapped the knife from my hand and put one paw on my chest. The lion pinned me to the ground, and the weight of the lion's foot on my chest made it hard to breathe.

"Santo!" I yelled at the top of my lungs.

The lion roared in my face, the hot breath I will never forget.

"Finish me!" I yelled at fur and fang. I could not move as the lion looked deep into my eyes and held me down.

"Who are you?" a still small voice asked in my mind. The chaos seemed quiet now. Again, "Who are you?" The question was much louder now as the sunlight seemed to illuminate this lion.

We stared at each other, and the lion drooled on me. I could feel my heartbeat thump violently, like a dead man being reborn. I looked up from the ground. The dust tried to settle as the lion was intrigued by me. His tail flicked. He almost smiled.

Suddenly, Santo appeared and knocked the lion off of me and to the ground. They went to fighting. I tried to stand, but collapsed from the pain. The roars and barks were constant, so I finally stood on one leg with all the effort only to be knocked down by the lion and Santo. Santo yelped behind me, and the lion roared. Just a few more steps and my rifle would be in my hands. Santo barked! The lion roared!

Santo could not survive against a five-hundred-pound lion much longer. I reached for my rifle in the tall grass as the fight became silent. I turned with my weapon and readied to kill a man-eating lion. I was shocked at what I saw.

The dust settled as the two stared at each other face to face, almost touching noses. Santo had several good claw marks on him, and the lion was missing a piece of his ear. They both were bloody and panting for oxygen. I put my sights on the lion's head, but I doubted as the lion looked at me and Santo whined, his tail wagging.

"Santo," I said out loud, keeping my rifle ready and trying to get my dog away from the lion. "Santo."

The gun was still prepared to fire. He would not obey me. The lion and dog were having a silent conversation without me. The lion began to purr as Santo's tail wagged. Santo then jumped up and down. He began to lick the lion on his face. The lion softly began to bring Santo closer to him and rubbed his head softly against the dog.

I was speechless, and the weapon was made safe. The lion turned to me with a grunt and disappeared into the thicket. I waited to see if Santo would follow.

"Santo!" I yelled again. He looked back one time and barked as he followed the lion into the unknown. The darkness of the lion's thicket swallowed them. The limbs and bushes shook one last time as the two disappeared.

I fell to my knees and wept. "Who are you?" I cried uncontrollable tears. It was hard to breathe. I could not help but look around to see if someone saw me crying. I felt warmth from my head to my toes, I felt loved.

"Who am I?" I cried. "I am a murderer!" I yelled as the tears rolled off of my face onto the ground. I could not stop. "I have killed. I have stolen."

The lion stuck his head out of the thicket and called softly as my heart ached. Our eyes connected as he disappeared back into the thicket with Santo beside him. "Wait."

I knelt in this tall grass and wept like a child as a black butterfly landed on my hand. Its actions calmed me, and after a brief moment, I regained my composure. I pushed myself up with my right leg and began the walk home. I walked much slower, but I could limp back home.

The occasional barks from Santo could be heard behind me as I limped home.

The house could be seen up ahead not far now as the sounds of a hammer and nail drowned out Santo's bark. The whole fence row and gate were now brand new. A solid wood frame gate must have cost Mamaw a fortune. I could not wait to see what the changes looked like up close.

The posts were of giant cedar logs, and the fence rows were stunning. It was something out of a magazine.

"What in the world?" I limped up to the fence with no dog behind me. Immanuel put the barbed wire around the braces in the corner of the fences and drove a nail into place.

"I see you met Papa." He struggled to get the last bit of barbed wire to hold but finally stood up and wiped the sweat from his forehead. He motioned for me to come closer and admire the work.

"How did you do this in such a short amount of time?" I asked.

"Um, magic señor," he said, laughed, and looked around for Santo. "I see Santo was willing to submit and be taught," Immanuel said as I limped past him through the vast and beautiful wooden gate.

"Why didn't the lion kill me?" I asked.

"As I said before, my friend, Papa has waited a long time for this, and heaven calls it mercy!" Immanuel laughed and slapped me on the shoulder.

"Papa has left his mark on you." Immanuel dropped his tools to take a look.

"Do not slap the other shoulder. I think there are teeth marks in that one," I reminded him.

"Okay, let me look at you." Immanuel stood right in front of me.

"Yep, can I go take a nap now and eat something?" I asked.

"Um, no," he replied quickly. "Your subconscious had associated pain with Papa. That is not how we do things around here. Papa is good, merciful, and powerful," he expressed himself.

"So?" I asked.

Immanuel touched my forehead and then my heart. It felt like someone poured warm oil on my head, and it ran down to my toes. I was so overcome with joy that physical healing was not noticeable, but I stood on both legs. My forearm and leg were made new. "What is happening?" I asked with tears running down my face.

"You are using emotions for the first time in a long time, my friend," Immanuel said before he hugged me and returned to work, as my body trembled uncontrollably.

"John, come and sit down and let's talk." Mamaw placed the blueberry muffins on the back porch table and poured the black coffee, just how I liked it. I took a step forward and noticed my healed body. The marks of a beast were gone.

I stretched my arms and legs in disbelief. "What did you do to me?" I asked while taking my seat under the porch. I reached out and collected my coffee, and leaned my gun against the wood rack.

"We are sharing the secrets of heaven with you," Immanuel said.

CHAPTER 8

"I almost forgot," Mamaw said as she jumped up and ran inside to grab the picture off the wall. The muffins and coffee were already placed in neat order on the back porch table before us.

"So, you're a murderer," Immanuel said in a nonchalant tone from across the yard, staring at the skinning post. I quickly turned to make sure my Mamaw did not hear that.

"It's more complicated than that," I said, having little desire to expose that part of my life.

"Yes, I suppose that death always is," Immanuel replied. I couldn't tell from his voice if he was being sarcastic or if he really meant it. At first, I assumed he was judging me, but there was something deeper than that.

He rubbed his wrists and that was when I noticed something I hadn't seen before.

A scar on each side. Like puncture wounds that might never fully heal. The unspoken truth of his identity lingered in the air and I knew it with certainty. The scars screamed of his sacrifice.

"Was it worth it?" I asked from the covered porch where I sat.

"Yes, every ounce of pain was worth it." Immanuel looked down at his scars for just a moment, then his gaze seared in my direction.

"Why did you go through all of that pain?" I asked as Immanuel was in deep thought and then smiled.

71

"So, you could walk out into the wild and meet a lion." He smiled and went back to his work.

I leaned back in the seat, thought about his response, and enjoyed the cup of coffee.

"I am just delighted you're here, and we have so much to talk about." My Mamaw set the painting down on the porch where all could admire it. "There, just a little more to the left, perfect. Now we can begin," she insisted.

"This is wonderful." I admired the scenery of the farm life and the food placed in front of me.

"Well, the berries were picked off my blueberry bush over yonder past the pigpen." She pointed towards her small vineyard.

"Hey, my leg and forearm are okay," I said.

Immanuel replied back quickly, "Enjoy it. You have another time with the lion really soon; you will need your running legs."

"Now, are we ready?" She pulled her glasses down for a better look at me.

"Fire at will." I grabbed a muffin from the basket.

"So tell me what you think this painting means," she insisted.

"I heard you say, blessings come from possessing nothing, or something close to that. Well, I wanted to possess everything, control it and make it mine. That selfish behavior is deep in my heart, almost captivating my every move, maybe because growing up, I had nothing," I said.

"What emotions did you feel in your search away from this place?" She took a sip of her coffee.

"Despair and loneliness, with a dark cloud that lingered over my head," I said quickly.

"What do you see about the house, the old shack?" she asked.

"The large beautiful windows? That had to be a way of seeing out, and the beautiful door was large for coming and going. The owners put more energy into the windows and front door than the whole house. Oh, and the flowers. Who would spend that kind of money on flowers?" I asked. "There was not an expensive item anywhere in the yard. The owner placed all of their possessions into what people would say was a waste of time and finances. With the money they spent on all of those flowers, big windows, and doors, you could at least have a decent vehicle to drive." I gnawed on my bottom lip in concentration.

"So, in the pursuit of everything, we may find nothing?" she asked, while I glanced out past that gate leading to the tall grass of a field, wanting another shot at the lion. "John, that led you here, to this place?" my Mamaw asked.

"That letter you sent me while in boot camp, my only letter," I replied.

"You came here with everything. Did you find nothing?" She had gotten up from her seat to check on a few flowers.

"I found something." I paused and watched the wind move the tall grass in the pasture. "You know if I called the police to report a lion, how bad would I be laughed at?" I wondered.

"In the pursuit of Heaven, be prepared to be laughed at," she chuckled. "It is more like you came here with nothing, and in your pursuit, you found something—a new beginning."

She watched me wonder quietly in thought. The black butterfly floated across the backyard and perched on the back of Immanuel's donkey.

"So, the house in the painting is somebody's soul?" I asked. She clapped and laughed softly, the evidence of her approval.

"The teacher has taught the student," she said, then walked over to me and kissed me on the forehead.

"A soul that is empty of possessing everything has a different way of seeing in and out than most people. Their life will be blessed and colorful. Their heart will not be consumed with despair and loneliness. When a man is down to nothing, Papa is up to something. The question you really want to ask is how will you respond the next time a lion calls you out?" she said. "Will you submit like Santo and spend quality time with Papa, or still practice your independence like most people?" she asked.

"John, we drink wine tonight," Immanuel said from across the yard while he measured the stalls on the barn that needed to be updated.

"Is it the good stuff?" I asked while he laughed.

"Lots of good to celebrate," he said as he returned to his work. "God is pleased with you."

"So, can a rich man enter heaven?" I asked her.

"Depends what is in his heart," she replied back very quickly. "If the center of his heart is his possessions, how can he?" my Mamaw asked as I cringed a little. I had a lot of money in Mexico that I really liked.

"John, lunch in two hours," she placed a spare set of truck keys on the table. "In case you need to go to town anytime while you are living here."

"Thanks." I wanted some work done on my M1. "I saw a sign a few miles back about a gunsmith. I want to update that rifle I bought from you."

"Go talk to him. He has been in business for a long time. Bill is his name." That was all Mamaw said as I gathered my rifle. I could hear a dog bark as I placed my things in that old Ford, but it was not Santo. I paused to study what I saw. A little truck came down the driveway and parked.

The bark was not from Santo but of a German Shepherd. The dog constantly barked in circles, and the truck swayed side to side a little. A petite female stepped out of the car with her hair in a ball cap. She was cute and had a nice figure and we locked eyes.

"Is Mamaw here?" She tried to talk over the barking dog, I snapped my fingers, and the dog sat down.

"Yes, she is here." I reached my hand out to introduce myself. "John Hunt."

The young lady giggled.

"Maddie." She shook my hand, and then grabbed some tomato plants in the back of the truck and walked to the front door.

"My precious calf-rescuer," my Mamaw said when she opened the front door. "That momma cow hates her own calf, never seen anything like it," Mamaw said as Maddie hugged her, still holding two tomato plants.

"Will the calf take a bottle?" Maddie asked.

"Just barely, baby, not even a pint of milk this morning."

"Did the momma kick her calf?" Maddie asked.

"Sadly, I think she did. The calf won't even try to get up and walk around."

"Why won't the calf try and drink a bottle?" I butted in, trying to be a part of the conversation; the two ladies turned to listen to me.

Mamaw placed her hands on her hips, "John, a little bit of rejection goes a long way, especially to something young." A knife pierced my heart, and I bit my lip. Silently, I turned and left them.

The gunsmith was only a few miles down the road, and after a brief conversation about war and politics, I returned to the farm. I sat in the truck for a few minutes.

I could see Maddie. She stared at me from the corral where the cow and calf were penned up as I passed by her. I had eyes in the back of my head, and I knew when someone watched me. Maddie was interested and I stopped dead in my tracks with my heart beating fast.

"Maddie, I'm glad you're here." I turned my eyes to meet hers. "I have not got the slightest clue on how to live the farm life." I laughed, and she smiled. I reached for the front door and went inside.

My Mamaw giggled, "I always hoped she would find a husband."

I wanted to look out the window and gaze at Maddie, just curious about the new face on the property. I stretched my neck around the corner to see outside, but I could not see her. I rushed to the back door and pulled it open.

"Do you want to live or die?" Maddie asked loudly from the barn. Immanuel nudged me over in that direction with his eyes. He had stained the new gate.

"Go serve," he turned back to his work as I fidgeted with a splinter in my hand.

I walked past the smelly pig pen and opened the gate to enter the barn. Maddie had the calf laid on a square bale of hay and tried to get the black bull calf to stand. The momma calf was at the other end of the small barn ten yards away and would not hardly even look at her calf. "How come that momma cow isn't doing this?" I asked while Maddie tried to get the calf to take a bottle.

Maddie was startled and dropped her bottle for the calf. "Oh gosh, sorry." She collected her thoughts and took a break. Her face was flushed and sweaty.

"Do you want some water?" I asked.

"No, thank you, I am about to go inside, and we can all have some. I have been at it for almost an hour. The calf doesn't want to live and has given up. The mom kicked him when he tried to nurse. The calf is hurt inside and out." She finished, took a breath of air, and pointed to a bump on the calf's head.

I felt my anger rising as my heart ached. I stared at that mother cow, and I wanted my knife, "I should cut your throat and watch you bleed." I walked towards that cow confidently. Her black eyes and mine connected. She put her head down and backed into a corner, and pawed the ground.

Maddie got up and moved to the gate. "I am thirsty now. Will you go have some tea with me?" Maddie removed herself from the tense situation.

I shook my head to clear my mind.

"Sure!" I walked backward, and I stopped to pet the calf who had eyes of despair. I picked up the bottle and set it on a beam for later as Maddie held the gate open for me. We walked together toward the back porch for a glass of tea.

"The calf hasn't taken the bottle. Soon the calf will die if it doesn't try to drink the colostrum," Maddie said.

"So, rejection is that bad," I added, but Maddie didn't say a word, only looked at me with a broken smile as we walked side by side. The back door to the house opened, and Mamaw sat two glasses down, full of ice, and a pitcher full of sweet tea.

"I'll get the sandwiches and chips for y'all." My Mamaw disappeared back into the house as we took our seat under the back porch, and pulled our chairs to the table.

Maddie poured our glasses in a giddy way. She was interested in my friendship for sure, but I was uncertain about her. I had never sought the companionship of a woman, only their bodies. My awkwardness was evident in her presence.

"Immanuel, come eat with us." I tried to break the silence.

"No, señor, I have to finish here today. Enjoy yourself." He bowed as Mamaw returned momentarily with the chips and placed them around us, and gave Maddie and me a kiss on the forehead. The backdoor was left open as her cat lingered in the entrance. My anger was still aroused from the cow at the barn.

"Get out of here, skunk," I said. I leaned forward in my seat and made a quick movement to scare that cat back inside, who hissed and ran. It was more a show of power to Maddie, who only laughed at me. She was not impressed. Maddie was pretty, but I did not feel any emotions toward her at that moment.

"You are different from most girls." I took a drink of tea and savored the turkey sandwich. Maddie had only eaten a few chips and held her tea glass with her spare hand.

"What do you mean?" Maddie asked curiously.

"Well, you could be doing, you know, girly stuff," I said weirdly.

"Well, maybe you don't know everything," she laughed and leaned forward to grab her sandwich. I realized she was much more intelligent than I gave her credit for. "I will come back after supper tonight and try to feed the calf." She tried to hide her food in her mouth while she talked.

"I look forward to it; maybe the calf will change his mind and decide to live," I said. We finished up our lunch as the phone rang. My Mamaw slid the backdoor open.

"Telephone, John Hunt."

"Excuse me." I stepped inside the house. "Hello," I grabbed the telephone off the coffee table in the den.

"This is Bill, I have your M1 Garand finished. It looks brand new."

"Already done in a couple of hours," I said, surprised.

"It was an honor, and I pushed your order forward. I already had a match-grade barrel and a complete stock set in inventory, and then I tuned the trigger. The operating rod needed lubrication, and I cleaned the gun very well. I hit the steel plate at six hundred yards on the third shot. Do you want to sell this gun?" he laughed.

"No, I am anxious to get it back. I am on my way," I said.

"Well, I had to ask," Bill added.

"I will bring you a few jars of homemade jam, and you will forget about that gun by tomorrow," I said as the conversation came to an end.

Maddie had finished up her lunch as I returned. I sat down to finish mine as well, but quickly.

"My M1 is ready to be picked up, and I am about to leave," I said. Maddie blew a sigh upward and caused her hair to blow with her breath as her hair fell down in front of her face just in time to give me that look of, please don't go. My heart pounded like a dead man being shocked and brought to life. I am sure my eyes told a similar story.

I dismissed myself and walked to the truck quickly. I looked back to wave at Maddie; she waved back and got up from her chair to go inside with Mamaw. Immanuel walked over to the garage where the truck was parked.

"I did not come to the farm to fall in love," I said. "I needed a new start."

"You wanted to find peace," he said, waving his hand over the dead flowers around the bottom beam that were beaten down from the previous work as I watched them come alive with radiant colors. "Life is one continuous process, John, of learning to let go," Immanuel said. "Forgiving your parents will help you form functional relationships, my friend. You're learning how to walk out and walk through your hurts."

"Oh wow, those flowers are beautiful; I have a place for these." Maddie walked over and pulled out a pair of scissors from her back pocket. "You never know when you might need to cut the stems of flowers," she cut a handful of radiant-colored flowers and skipped back inside, only stopping at the backdoor of my Mamaw's house to wave at me.

I watched Maddie, and I missed her even for just a moment. She also wore those jeans just right. I shook my head and cleared my throat with Immanuel not twenty feet away.

"We need to talk about those flowers," I said to my Mexican friend as I shut the door on that old Ford.

"Maddie would love to talk about those flowers with you, señor," he smiled. "The more you get to know her, your kindred spirits will find each other," he pointed at me with a craftsman's level as I pulled out of the driveway.

The gun shop was at the edge of town, and I could hear the rifle fire that came from behind the building. I now understood why there was no house in sight, and the driveway was long. That guy liked his space. The front door was locked, which caused me to go to the back of the gun shop.

"Mr. Bill," I hollered as the rifle fire stopped.

"Come on around, son," Bill said.

In his seventies, Mr. Bill was a nice guy, with a calm demeanor, and knowledgeable. "Not many people turn me down completely when I offer to buy a gun," he said.

"Some things cannot be bought." I shook his hand. The M1 rested on a nearby table, along with several clips of full metal jacket loads. I smiled like a possum when I saw the weapon. I walked immediately over to pick it up.

The wood on the stock and forearm was brand new walnut, the barrel had a shiny bore, and the trigger felt good. "John, go ahead and put some rounds down range and see how you like it. The steel plate is 600 yards," Bill said.

"Don't mind if I do," I added.

I placed a full clip of eight rounds in the top and slammed the bolt shut with my right hand. I fired from a standing position, the bullet struck the plate the first shot at 100 yards, and sent a sharp ring in the report back to us. I fired at the closer targets, and rapidly hit them all six more times, some 200, and the others at 400 yards. My last round found the 600-yard steel plate as the bullet struck, and we waited for the report as the M1 made the distinctive ping of the clip being ejected out the top.

"Brings back memories," Bill spat his tobacco on the ground. "That is impressive son. What do you do for a living?" Bill asked with curiosity in his voice. I thought for a second before answering.

"I do contract work overseas," I answered before handing Bill his money. He followed me back to my truck.

"Hey, Bill?"

"Yes, son, what is on your mind?" he replied rather quickly while I set my gun inside the truck.

"How do you know you met a special girl?" I asked while I reached for the truck door.

"When your spirit is kindred with hers, you will know."

I waved goodbye as I cranked the truck and came home.

Santo had not yet returned home when I parked that old Ford under the garage at my Mamaw's house. Maddie was not there and the sun was behind the trees signaling the day was ending. Immanuel was not outside, but every light at my Mamaw's house was on.

As I entered the back door after I parked the truck, I stopped to hear Santo's bark way off in the distance. I knew he was coming home soon. The smell coming from the kitchen caused me to forget everything else that happened that day. I stopped to peek into the open doors of the kitchen. I held my M1 Garand like a preacher holds his Bible.

Immanuel poured red wine in a glass for himself as my Mamaw danced around freely in the spirit and snacked on the meats, cheeses, and pieces of bread that covered the countertop beside the coffee maker. The kitchen was decorated with sunflowers everywhere.

"Maddie picked these before she left and decorated in here. She said she wanted to be here but could not. I just love her so much. It would be nice if she was in my family." Mamaw winked at me.

"You keep drinking that wine." I smiled.

"My friend, when you put your things away, come and join us," Immanuel said as he presented a clean wine glass and set it on the counter for me, and bowed gently. There was food everywhere, some things I had never seen before. The smells were magnificent. The fragrance of Heaven was all I could think about if I was to describe it.

"Maddie tried to feed that calf, but he just didn't want to eat today," my Mamaw said. That was sad news, and I went upstairs and put my things away. I could hear the two talking as I made my way upstairs. I contemplated the day's events while soaking in a hot shower.

I turned off the water and stepped out before wiping the condensation off the mirror above the sink. I took a good look at myself, my reflection. If I could go back in time, would I make changes? The answer was yes, but to avoid my time there, would have been foolish. That place was somewhere beyond fantasy, a long look past a mystery for sure. A lion who spoke from his mind, breathing being of blood and bone who knew my deepest sins.

"Who are you?" I looked at my own reflection and wondered when the lion would come for me.

"John Hunt," my Mamaw yelled from the bottom of the stairs. "Your food and company are waiting." There was no use answering her. She would only start a conversation from downstairs and prolong my stay in that bathroom.

I eased the door open and peaked out. No lion waited outside the bathroom door. I was a little thankful, but disappointed. But candles were lit in the living room, almost like beacons for a ship that sailed at night. Once again, I was guided to her kitchen, and two faces smiled and waited for me.

"Papa is excited for you and your courage to face the things of your past. Be delighted in his goodness. This was all his idea. I am his servant," Immanuel bowed again.

The breath of Papa blew around the room, giving me chills up and down my spine.

"His Spirit is with us," my Mamaw said in a loud proclamation of joy. "He is always so close," she said as a tear was wiped from her face. She reached out her hand to draw me into the kitchen for our time of fellowship.

I wanted to ask where the lion was, but Immanuel saw the question forming in my mind.

"Papa is with Santo still. Who is going to return soon." He walked over to the counter to grab some fresh bread and cheese to go with his wine.

81

"So, now the doors to the kitchen have been opened to me. I was not allowed in here before that." I spoke a little loud.

"Yep," my Mamaw butted in as she stirred a pot on the stove. "There are secrets even in Heaven, and unbelief is not allowed," she said excitedly.

"Like the lion in the thicket," I added, taking a sip of the new wine. "Why the lion, not some other way?" I asked.

"This is where I come in," Immanuel adjusted a sunflower that was on the counter resting in a vase. "Because of your past, Heaven knew that a display of Power and Mercy would be the only way to reach you. You searched for power the wrong way, and you have never really given out mercy in your life. The lion is a representation of those two acts."

"Wait." My Mamaw raised her hand like a kid in school. The silence was awkward, but that was how she liked it, with the tick-tock of the giant clock in the hallway. She breathed out a sigh of relief, "You're right, go on. I just thought I was going to prove you wrong." She filled her wine glass from the bottle that rested on the counter while giggling.

"As I was saying," Immanuel said. "God meets you in a place where you could be reached. Your perception of power is flawed because of your past, creating a place for mercy to find you, and you needed a physical and visual aid; therefore, a lion was sent from above," Immanuel said.

I gave a silent whistle of uncertainty. "It really is peaceful out here." I walked over to the counter and sampled the delicious food spread out.

"John, take a deep breath because this is going to hurt," Immanuel said as I was stuffing my face.

"How can this hurt? I have never tasted cheese and bread this good. Well, the time I was shot up, and you fed me on that mountain. Is this another serious moment? Am I going to cry again?" I smiled with my mouth full.

"Finish your food," Mamaw placed a hand on my face as I looked at them. I could sense that something was about to happen.

"I am much more than just a man," Immanuel said. I looked at my Hispanic friend with an act of faith. "It is time you discover that," he told me, placing an arm around my neck in a display of comfort.

"I have never really had any real friends," I confessed as I fought the urge to push him away.

"Or a brother," Immanuel paused as Mamaw put her other arm around me, circling me in a giant hug of affection.

"This is going to hurt, John." Immanuel had tears roll down his face. "You have a recurring dream that is about to be finished. Be brave and face the hurts of your childhood." Immanuel comforted me and patted my face as the tears swelled in my eyes. My Mamaw held on tight as the calendar on the wall directly in front of me began to roll the months back October, September, August, May, and January, and the calendar soared off the wall with a flash of light.

CHAPTER 9

The dream began like always. The boy sat under the tree, isolated, scared, and lonely, his eyes and posture—abandonment and rejection, the image of my younger self. As we made visual contact, the boy reached out to me. I grabbed his hand and pulled him upright; maybe I was there to help him.

I felt an instant flow of heartache and despair as I grabbed his hand. Tarnished memories rushed through my soul. The things in the dark rumbled to the light. The boy and I were attached through time. Our touch connected us as if we were yoked together. I do not remember that look of total disconnect from the real world. I tried to walk, to lead him away from the dead tree, but I collapsed. My muscles lacked the strength. As the little boy gripped my hand with intensity and passed his pain to me, my knees had become weak. The load was too heavy.

"Immanuel" was the only name I knew that could help me.

As the boy loosed his grip on my hand, he yawned like a bear going into slumber for the winter. The sun began to set on the horizon. I looked around and hoped something of Heaven would appear. I nudged him.

"Hey."

The boy had fallen asleep and was unresponsive as I wept uncontrollably in the dead brown grass under that tree. I still held his hand. He wouldn't wake up, even after I shook him. He was lifeless.

A thought ran through my mind to ask for help again as I wept even harder.

"Immanuel, I need your help," I screamed. I tried to carry the boy's body, but I could not pick up the lifeless corpse. The load was too much to take alone. "Immanuel!" I yelled.

I was exhausted. I fell to the grass, leaving the boy only feet away. The vegetation around me was dry, and bones of the dead were scattered to-and-fro. I was about to give up. I laid down in defeat. I rested my exhausted face into the dead grass and took big breaths of air, and tried to recover on my own. This dream had never gone this far. I wanted to be back at the farm and out of this nightmare.

"May I try, my friend?" a familiar voice offered as a hand was placed on my shoulder. I picked my head up from the ground and looked into the kind eyes of my companion, my savior. "I bet, if you let me, I can carry the both of you," Immanuel laughed, kneeling down to look me in the eyes as I wallowed in despair and shame. I tried to stand. I fell, but I felt joy every time my companion smiled. Immanuel's face shone brightly, and his disposition was radiant.

"I tried to save him, to wake him," I cried, but managed to find my feet.

"Papa has a different plan for you, John." My friend reached down with ease and picked up the boy that slumbered. The body was lifeless and limp as Immanuel held him in his left arm.

"This is a part of your life that needs to be buried so you can move on," Immanuel said and looked at me directly in the eyes. "As long as you are connected to the hurts of your childhood, you will not be able to move on into something greater."

Immanuel reached out to me and placed his other arm around my waist, picking me up and giving me strength. He patiently steadied my weak legs as I put my feet down to stand.

"This is the part that is going to really hurt. Papa needs you to bury your rejection," my companion suggested.

"Should I take a deep breath?" I asked Immanuel.

"No, John, just courage," he squeezed my hand. "We have watched you since birth. This is a joyous time for us. Papa is pleased with you," he said.

That made me cry again.

"Hey." I looked down at the ground as the dead brown grass came alive under my feet. The bones came to life and turned into a herd of deer that galloped on the horizon, stopping to graze on the clover just up ahead. The scattered bones and flowers began to grow richly and brightly all around us.

Even the branches on the single tree I noted earlier began filling with green leaves. Color blossomed before my eyes.

"It begins, my friend because we make all things new" Immanuel looked at the boy and let go of me for just a moment, touching the sides of the boy's face and neck.

"What are you doing?" I asked him.

"Preparing the body, Señor John. I was waiting for him to fall asleep forever." Immanuel placed the boy on the ground while whispering words over the body. I watched as Immanuel revealed a white cloth from under his shirt. He spread out the fabric and placed the boy in a position for burial. Immanuel took his time and gently folded the corners inward and then across.

"Grab the shovel next to the tree," Immanuel insisted.

"Shovel?" I said curiously, looking around, and finally tripped over it almost falling down. "First day with my new feet," I laughed.

Immanuel began to laugh with me. "See, John, you are already having fun," he said as I grabbed the shovel with some authority.

"I will give you strength." Immanuel looked at me as he prepared the body. "This is something that you must do for yourself. We have prepared everything before and after today." He placed a hand on the boy's lifeless head. "And we will bury the body under the tree, pick a spot. When I finish preparing the body, I will join you," Immanuel said.

"I understand." I quickly found the place where the grass and flowers had not taken over. I glanced up; the size of the tree was much more significant now due to the sudden changes. I looked back to see Immanuel gather up some fresh flowers.

"Will the sins of my father continue through me?" I asked.

"Not after today, my friend. This is spiritual," he said. Immanuel poured a fragrance of some type over the body as I began to break the ground. I jabbed the shovel's blade into the ground, but to my surprise, it was much easier to dig in the dirt than I thought it would be. With every shovelful of dirt, my heart broke. I fought back tears with every thrust and tossed the soil into a pile close by.

"This was all His idea." Immanuel pointed to a hill covered in beautiful green grass, the highest place. The lion watched over us as I stood on my shovel and wiped tears away.

Immanuel moved the body closer, ready for burial, wrapped neatly in white garments.

"I wanted a father here. I just felt like I needed to say that."

"That is why Papa is here. He is just letting you know he is with you," Immanuel said.

Immanuel stopped tending the body to take a look at Papa. "He has been a great dad to me. I think he could be a good Papa to you as well, my friend," he suggested. I smiled. "Can I place the body to rest?" Immanuel asked politely.

"I want to do it," I said, brushing the sweat out of my eyes.

"Señor, just ask me, and I will help you," Immanuel said, placing the body in my hands and touching my arms with his fingers sending a bolt of lightning through my body. "My strength is in you now," he said, stepping back and giving me space; the body was as light as a feather.

My friend gently placed the body in the ground. "Thank you," I said, looking up at Immanuel, who bowed humbly. Looking down at the wrapped body, I could not see a face, but I stood, strengthened by what I was doing. I felt empowered.

"You will learn to think differently," Immanuel said, sprinkling some more flowers and more oil over the body.

My expression said it all. "Where do you keep all of this food, water, herbs, and spices?" I asked, and he laughed.

"So many things to learn, my friend," he replied as he reached and began to draw with his finger on the bark. "Be fruitful," he said as the tree began to give birth to the fruit it so longed for. "From this day forward, your life will be different." The fruit made a distinct sound when it fell to the ground, a thud.

"I am not a farmer, but doesn't fruit take several months to ripen, not two minutes?" I said, backing up to see what was happening.

"Now, my friend, your life will be even more prosperous than you could ever imagine. Your heart will be free. Look over to here," he said, pointing. Behind the tree was a vineyard full of fresh purple grapes. The vines were full and thick with fruit.

"One more thing to do," Immanuel insisted, as I was gazing out onto the new life being presented all around me.

"Oh yeah, the grave marker," I said, with a mouth full of fruit, and quickly grabbed the wooden cross bearing my old name, John Hunt. "I will be glad to do this," I said.

"On the third hit, my friend, hit it just right," Immanuel was encouraging me.

I tossed the fruit, spit in my hands for extra grip, and grabbed my shovel in my right hand and the grave marker in my left. With authority, I steadied the grave monument. One strike shook the ground, and the second split the clouds in two. Taking a quick glance at Immanuel, I drew the shovel back as high as my arms could support it; coming down quickly and with force, I found the perfect spot. The loud thud of metal striking wood brought me back to the kitchen, looking into the eyes of Immanuel and my beloved Mamaw.

"It is finished," I said, standing back home in that kitchen where God's presence seemed to dwell. The dream was over. The wind blew around the room, and I could feel Papa's spirit pass by, causing me to laugh sincerely so hard that I had to hold myself up. The joy was overwhelming and unspeakable.

"Papa is pleased with you, and your soul has found the true rest it has searched for," Mamaw said, giggling as she spoke the words of affirmation. Her laughter was contagious as Immanuel joined in.

"John, you have been healed. Now you have been surrounded by people and circumstances to help you establish your new life. You are still a fighter, but your heart will be different from this day forth," Mamaw said, placing her hands on my face to turn my eyes towards hers.

Immanuel refilled my glass of wine that was on the counter. The lion called from the darkness somewhere out in the tall grass of the pasture, maybe even the thicket.

"Man, that lion never sleeps nor slumbers," I said, grabbing my wine glass.

"He is jealous right now. He wants to be in here with us," Immanuel said, smiling. "Let the beast teach you," Immanuel said, looking out the window into the blackness but squeezing my shoulder to get my attention. Immanuel began to check his pockets in motion that he was about to leave.

"Are you calling it a night?" I asked, taking a sip of wine in a rich man's glass.

"Today was a good day, but I must go to my God and to your God, my Father and your Father," he said, grabbing his wine glass from the counter. "Walk with me, my friend, for a little bit," he said, looking at me but turning to face Mamaw and giving her a kiss on the cheek as she handed him some food for the evening.

"You might get hungry in the middle of the night," she said, placing bread and cheese sandwiches in his hand.

"Always thinking of others. That is why we are so fond of you," Immanuel said, hugging her.

Mamaw got so tickled, that she jumped up, leaving the ground a few inches. Her fart echoed in the kitchen, causing both of us to stop.

"Whoops, that cheese is rich," she said, taking another bite with a red face from the wine.

The smell was tainting the air as Immanuel and I covered our wine glasses but made it out the backdoor, quickly stepping onto the concrete patio.

"Well, I was left here with all this wine and cheese."

The calls from Papa were getting closer, stirring the farm animals. We walked together in the cool of the night as I went over the events of the day in my mind, not speaking, just wiping my nose on my shirt.

"You should tell Maddie about today," Immanuel suggested. I could see her standing in front of me. Her hair would be up, but those few strands would be dangling in front of her eyes, just right. There had never been a woman that could do that to me.

The lion continued to call somewhere out there. I kept looking out, hoping to see him in the darkness. The gate Immanuel built was spectacular; perfection could only describe it. We leaned on it together. I listened, even turning an ear towards the darkness. "What is Papa saying, roaring in that way? It is not a battle cry," I asked, but Immanuel waited a few seconds before answering.

"It's a beautiful invitation, John Hunt. He is saying, here I am, come to me. I will protect you, teach you, and tell you about myself. Heaven has secrets that are not just told to anybody," Immanuel said. I could hear the tremble in his voice. "Even I have to go talk to him, disappear a while with a lion," he added, taking the last sip of his glass of wine and giving it back to me to bring inside. "The farm allowed you to slow down and you heard Papa's voice. Not many people can hear his voice anymore".

"Thank you for saving my life in that valley," I said, knowing that he was about to leave.

"It was the reason I was born," he said, smiling halfway, tuning into what I was saying, looking out into the darkness. "Well, well, Santo has returned," Immanuel said, straining to see in the darkness of the night. I could hear the pants of a dog and the footsteps of something coming.

Immanuel opened the gate to let that Cur dog in who ran to get to his dog house. "Maybe I should get him some food and water. He seems tired," I said.

"He is full, Papa took care of him, Santo will sleep for a while, three days," Immanuel said, opening the gate enough so he could walk through. The calls of the lion were so close the animals except Santo were stirred. The sounds of Santo's tail hit the dog house. "Maddie would love to hear about your dream. She is a dreamer also," Immanuel said, before crossing over and closing the gate. He walked into the blackness towards the voice of his Father, who I could barely see.

The lion brushed himself against his son, who returned affection quickly. "John, Papa said your time is coming soon," my Hispanic friend said, but the lion was selfish for his time and wouldn't let him talk long without smothering Immanuel with affection. Pushing Immanuel with his head and wanting to play, swatting at Immanuel's heels, trying to trip him. The lion was so much bigger but desired the closeness of Immanuel, even licking his hands and rubbing his mane and muscular body constantly on the carpenter as they walked away and disappeared into the dark together.

As I held the glass of Immanuel and swallowed the remaining evidence of my own, the evening mosquitoes began to bother me. I turned to go back inside, stopping to look into the doghouse at Santo. The evening light of the house shined dimly, illuminating a tired dog who only made eye contact and a groan of exhaustion. He briefly looked up from his dog house only to yawn and fade away into the night. I could hear Santo snoring as I shut the backdoor. I passed the kitchen where Mamaw was cleaning up the last few dishes. I easily hand-washed the two wine glasses, rinsing them with hot water only and setting them to the side to dry.

"It has been a day for you, hasn't it?" she asked, wiping down her counters and moving a large distilling vat she had brewing more wine. "I really don't drink much wine until Heaven comes around," she said laughing, "but Immanuel loves it, so I keep some ready. "

"Sure," I said, rolling my eyes. "Santo is back. He is out cold sleeping," I added.

"I have some scraps for him in the morning. I am sure he is full right now. Papa always feeds well," she spoke, writing something on her wine vats distilling.

"Do you think the calf is going to make it?" I asked, changing the subject.

"The outcome is out of our control now. We just have to see if it will eat," Mamaw said, handing me a flashlight from a drawer inside the countertop. "One more try before bedtime. See if the calf will eat something. The bottle is sitting on a beam in the barn. Shake it before you try to feed the calf. The evenings have been warm, so the milk is still good," she said.

Retrieving the wine glass I had just put down, I filled the glass with water from the sink. I gulped down the water quickly, knowing I had a job to do. With the water dripping off my face, I set the glass down, leaving it for later.

"I will try," I sighed

"Exchange your anger for patience; this will be a good way to practice," she said, pushing me out of the kitchen as she picked up her black and white cat and walked me to the back door. "You like her, don't you?" she asked right before I walked outside.

"Like who?" I asked, winking at her. I stepped onto the concrete patio for what seemed like the hundredth time today. Santo never even looked at me but continued to sleep deeply, alone in his doghouse. Only his head was visible, and the rest of his body was wrapped in hay.

"Go serve," my Mamaw said, shutting the back door. The house lights were enough to get me onto the grass without twisting my ankle. Once I set foot onto the soft ground, my flashlight was needed, the light just enough to illuminate the path towards the barn.

"Dang it, the batteries are almost dead," I said to myself. I thought about going back to the house for more batteries but decided I could finish this job within ten minutes and be in bed.

The gate to the barn was easy to find. I could hear the momma cow walking around. She was spooked to have something moving so close to her this late at night. The flashlight though dimness, illuminated her black body and eyes. She quickly moved to the opposite end of the corral, where she and her calf stayed. I thought that Maddie would be proud of me if I could get this calf to eat.

The momma cow was angry, pawing the ground a few yards away, not protective of her baby, just plain crazy. I shined my light on her, wishing she would try to charge. I would end her life in a second with whatever tool I could find.

"It's your choice to do this," I said, turning my back to look for the calf. I just completely ignored the problem behind me, wanting to stomp me to the ground.

I searched the hay on the north side of the corral in the covered area looking for the rejected calf. Maybe he would take some milk. The bottle was on the beam that I had just walked past, and I spotted it with the dim light. There was food and water for the momma cow if she wanted to eat, also in buckets.

"I hope you choke," I spoke when I noticed she had been eating and drinking very well.

I spotted the calf in a corner all by himself, and I pitied what I found. His eyes looked lifeless when I found him, I tried to get him to stand, but he collapsed under fatigue. After setting the flashlight down and retrieving the bottle, I tried to get the calf to feed. Even forcing his mouth open, he would not eat anything. The milk would just run out of the sides of his mouth.

The routine began with putting the flashlight down that was about to run out of battery with a dim light and picking up a bottle to try and force food down the calf's throat; it turned into a twenty-minute circus. The sweat from my arms and forehead collected every dust particle in that barn.

My emotions ran low, only to find anger that something so easy was made into the impossible. One last time, I shined the light into the calf's eyes. The cloudy eyes were faded. I remember Maddie saying that it's terrible when the eyes go from black and glossy to gray and cloudy. The calf was about to die.

The light on my flashlight just burned out suddenly while I held the little calf's head up. The milk in the bottle was all over me and empty. I was tired from twenty minutes of this. My anger was rising. I knew I had to walk away. I could hear that momma cow drinking water and eating feed without a care in the world. She was completely disconnected from her calf.

"Your baby is about to die, and you won't even feed it. How could you be so selfish?" I asked with wrath in my voice.

I gently laid the calf back into the hay and I stood. The cow sensed my aggression as I turned to face it. She was small but could hurt a man. I walked toward her, tossing the bottle at her feet to test her reaction. She moved forward.

"Yep, you are crazy," I said. "When your calf dies, maybe you can look at it for a long time. It will give you something to think about." The cow began to paw the ground wanting to fight. "I am going to make a burger out of you," I said.

The cow lunged forward, causing me to throw the flashlight at her striking the beam above her. She stopped long enough for me to land a right fist on the side of the head. The cow staggered backward into a beam shaking the covered area of the corral. As the cow staggered around the barn, trying to regain its composure, I calmly walked back to the house, closed the gates behind me, and went back inside.

"Well, what did you learn?" Mamaw asked as she was knitting something, sitting in the living room. I walked by, shaking my hand.

"I learned that a cow's head is hard, and I might have broken something," I said before Mamaw butted in.

"You missed Maddie," she said, grinning at me.

"I said I missed Maddie's help out there," I insisted wholeheartedly as I flexed my right hand over and over, trying to work out the pain that was going away slowly. "I think it will be bruised. I don't feel anything broken," I said while trying to go upstairs.

"Immanuel will be back in the morning, maybe Maddie also," she said, turning off the light by her living room chair. The cat jumped down from his perch and followed her to the bedroom. My Mamaw kissed me on the forehead, "Goodnight, John."

CHAPTER 10

The rooster's crow seemed louder, reminding me to get up and start my day.

I wanted to stay in bed and not walk outside to the barn to find a dead calf. I did not want to face the rejection of the natural. My emotions were saying to avoid that day at all cost, but I knew this had to be done.

"John," my Mamaw called from downstairs. "Pancakes and bacon," she said at the edge of the stairs that led to my upstairs room. I stood to my feet, stretched, and went to the window. I could see the cow in the corral eating hay. Her tail flicked in contentment as a mockingbird walked on the railing beside her. I could not see the calf, but I bit my lip as I stared.

"I really do want to shoot you right between the eyes," I said to the source of my aggravation. My M1 Garand was next to me, locked and loaded. I grabbed a clean shirt and pants, then down the stairs, I went.

The kitchen doors were wide open. I peeked around the corner and hoped to see a lion.

"Here you go, baby." My Mamaw handed me a cup of coffee, and her smile was as bright as always.

"What are you looking for, John?" she asked, fixing my plate of food.

"Purpose," I answered quickly, but slowly I turned to look outside and hoped to see a black calf walking around in the corral linked to the barn. Santo's head appeared from his doghouse, and I swear he smiled at me also. I returned the smile and Santo fell back to his slumber.

"Life is one big opportunity," Mamaw laughed and brought my plate to the table. I stared at my food, not really all that hungry, and clutched my coffee cup for comfort. "The first step is always the hardest," Mamaw said as she knew I did not want to check on the calf. "Love puts us in a place to be hurt, but the hurts are few and far between. Lots more joy in our lives when we try to love." She reached out to hold my hand. I took a bite of food that did not taste good and quickly put my fork down.

"Maybe I can eat this later," I suggested.

"Don't worry about it. I'll put the plate in the microwave later for some warm-ups when your appetite comes back." Mamaw smiled. I took several sips of coffee before I began my day.

"Before I start my workday, I need to make a phone call. I need some money." I walked into the living room and searched for a pen and paper. "I will do something for myself today," I suggested.

The landline phone was on the kitchen wall, so I pulled up a stool and took a seat beside it. I punched in the numbers of my bank in Mexico. The conversation took several minutes, with passwords and bank account information in Spanish. I was oblivious to Immanuel, who stepped in through the backdoor.

"Eighty-thousand dollars, my friend, is a lot of money," Immanuel said out loud as I finalized the arrangement in Spanish. I listened to the lady giving me the last details, confirmed my order, and tried to keep her from hearing Immanuel's voice.

"What, eighty thousand dollars?" My Mamaw clutched her heart and got up from the table to grab her own pen and paper. She began to write, from what I could see, fervently. I smiled.

Immanuel leaned over her shoulder and began to chuckle.

"Me and my big mouth, sorry, Señor." He filled his coffee cup and walked back outside to start work. As I hung the phone up, a note was placed in my hand.

"Since you are a millionaire, we could use these things around the house," she said as her eyes never looked so big.

I unfolded the note. "A new truck, a roof, new kitchen appliances, washer and dryer, and one hundred head of Beefmaster cattle with the land cleared and fenced." Mamaw had moved to the window and day-dreamed for a second.

"And feed and hay for the cows," she added.

"Wow," I tapped my foot on the floor. I had forgotten about the calf briefly. "How about thirty head of cattle, and the land cleared and fenced? That will take several months to obtain." I stuck out my hand for her to shake. She shook my hand quickly and hugged me so hard my back popped.

"Go and deal with your rejection. I have to get my cattle buying clothes ready." Mamaw went to her bedroom to change, and I was left briefly alone in the kitchen. I cleared my head and thought about breakfast, but changed my mind. I stopped at the back door and wondered about bringing my gun just in case. I waited; briefly, the phone rang, and Mamaw returned downstairs to answer it.

"Maddie, he's going to check on the calf now," I heard Mamaw say. I slowly fidgeted with a picture on the wall and straightened a few chairs around just so I could listen to the last part of the conversation, hoping Maddie could come by for a visit. I did not want to sound evident that I was interested in Maddie. "I am making dinner for you if you want to stick around. Green beans, cornbread, and fried deer steak," I heard Mamaw say as my heart leaped in my chest. It hurt a little, but this time I liked it.

The hinges made an unforgettable squeak as I left the security of Mamaw's house and walked toward the corral. The pigs and chickens stood and followed me with their eyes. They knew something was wrong.

I opened the corral gate and spotted the calf, lifeless and alone. The mother cow flicked her tail in aggravation at me and pawed the ground.

"This was your choice." I took my eyes away from the calf that lay in the corner, lifeless. "I should put a bullet in your head for starving this calf like this." I looked her in the eye.

I slowly walked toward the calf and kneeled down to rub his soft fur. Instead, I was met with a cold and stiff, lifeless body.

"I am sorry, I did the best I could, I tried," I preached. I thought I was alone as the momma cow began to pace frantically around the corral. "No, I am not going to kill you." Her black eyes were set on mine. She put her head down and stared. I stepped forward to meet her halfway.

"Give him to us," a familiar voice said from behind me. I stopped.

"I was going to haul the calf off to the boneyard, and let the coyotes have him." My hand still hurt from punching that cow yesterday.

"Papa would love to have it." Immanuel walked over to the dead calf.

"Could you bring him back from the dead?" I asked.

"Yes, but this rejection needs to be given to Papa, as your first offering," Immanuel said. "Some things do not need to be resurrected, John," he gently rubbed the fur of the little calf.

"What is Papa going to do with the calf?" I asked while rubbing the pain in my chest. Immanuel picked up the calf with ease.

"Consume it. I always enjoy bringing hurts and fears to Papa." Immanuel turned to walk towards the gate.

"Is that the reason you were born?" I asked curiously. Santo howled from the front porch and began to stroll towards the barn where we were. He was still sore from his run with the lion.

"When you find out why you were born, Señor, all of this will make more sense," Immanuel said. Santo walked to the gate with a limp and a whine.

"Are you about healed up?" I joked, looking at Santo, who yawned and leaned against my leg, begging for a scratch on the head as Immanuel opened the new gate leading to the pasture.

The sunshine burst through the clouds like a symphony. The rays made the calf glisten like glitter on the back of Immanuel's donkey. "How does it feel to give an offering unto Papa?" Immanuel asked me while securing the calf with rope.

"Different, but much easier than I thought. The burden is no longer mine to hold onto," I responded.

"Just like letting go, my friend, this is a constant process. Like all processes, the first step is the hardest and can be perfected with time," he spoke. The lion began to call Immanuel from his place of power. He wanted my rejection and my loss. "Your time with Papa is almost here, don't forget to submit when he stands before you," Immanuel said.

"Amen," I said, petting Santo, who was getting excited and jumped up on the gate, hoping he could catch a glimpse of his Papa, his friend. The lion would call out, a soft roar. Santo would answer with bark and long for another run with the lion.

"What is the lion doing, calling like that?" I asked Immanuel.

"He is searching for me," Immanuel said. Immanuel tapped the gate with his hand and turned away.

The walk back inside never seemed so easy. I guess my burden was lighter. Even before I put my foot on the back step, my hunger had returned, and the calf was forgotten.

"Woman, I think this was all planned," I said out loud and walked into the house, and turned the corner to the kitchen; there stood Maddie.

"Oh, sorry, I thought my Mamaw was here," I made an excuse.

Maddie had the pantry door open and her hand in a coffee container.

"Dark chocolate is my secret sin," she said, laughing.

I was shocked to see her.

"That is my favorite chocolate too." I scratched my head. "Mamaw never showed me her chocolate stash."

"What is the best thing to drink with dark chocolate?" Maddie chewed and tried to hide her chocolate-covered teeth.

I laughed, "Red wine, of course, also my favorite." Maddie agreed and reached over the counter to get a napkin and kicked one foot up. I noticed her body language change as she played with her hair; she liked me.

We heard footsteps coming down the hall and Maddie put the chocolates away quickly, as Mamaw returned.

"Now, the secret to a good gravy is to let it simmer. Your man will go crazy and be on you like white on rice." Mamaw looked surprised to see me. "Well, how did it go?"

"The calf didn't make it. I gave it to Immanuel. He took it out to the thicket so Papa could have it," I said. "I feel much better now," I admitted. I almost felt naked in front of Maddie.

"Now you're ready to get married," Mamaw walked over to the microwave to warm up my brunch.

"Maddie," she said out loud, who tried to hide her red face.

"Yes," Maddie said.

"So, do you have a boyfriend?" I asked Maddie, who smiled and changed the subject.

"So, who is Papa?" Maddie asked as I spilled tea all over myself.

"Papa is a lion that lives in a thicket just at the edge of the property. A lot is going on around here," I said while cleaning up my mess. "When he wants to, he will come out of the thicket, mostly he will come out to deal with a problem or to show himself. Immanuel took the dead calf to him as my first offering," I said. Maddie crossed her arms at the dinner table, trying not to be played for a fool.

"A Mexican guy named Immanuel took a dead calf to the lion. My Sunday school class would possibly disagree with you," Maddie smiled.

"The dead calf was loaded onto Immanuel's donkey, then taken to the lion." I smiled.

"So now there is a donkey?" Maddie asked as Mamaw slipped into the kitchen to clean the coffee pot. "Oh, I'm not going anywhere. I want to see this," Maddie said.

"Jesus!" Mamaw said and looked down at her arm. It was covered in chill bumps. She bowed her head in reverence to what was being spoken to her in silence. Maddie jumped in her seat like lightning and rubbed her hand down her arms, which were also covered in chill bumps.

"There is something special about to happen," Maddie looked at me. Mamaw was still silent. She lifted her head and looked at me as well from the kitchen, the place where God's spirit would manifest itself.

"Papa is coming for you," she said.

"I wish I could feel lightning bolts and chill bumps," I said as Maddie continued to laugh and the giggles hit my Mamaw again, something of the spirit.

The donkey's bray could be heard coming out of the tall grass as Immanuel and his donkey reappeared. I ran to the gate to meet him. We had much to talk about.

"So, Papa's joy has found those two," Immanuel said as I opened the gate to let him in before tying his donkey to the post. "Joy is something you will understand later. Right now, my friend, it's Papa's power and mercy that he wants to burn within your mind and soul. He doesn't want you to forget it along the way," Immanuel said.

"Burn me, eat me, I guess, whatever," I shrugged my shoulders. "How did the lion accept my offering?" I asked Immanuel.

"Papa ate your offering right in front of me; the days of your rejection are over," he said, bowing his head, then put a hand on my shoulder. "You are free to move on now." Immanuel tied his donkey to a post.

"That means a lot to me, the world," I said.

"You can tell the lion yourself, very soon. Your Mamaw felt it earlier when Papa spoke it to me out in the thicket just a few minutes ago. Papa likes to speak face to face. He loves you, Señor John, and Papa never intended to kill you. But he does like a good fight," Immanuel spoke with a grin.

"What does God's kindness look like?" I asked as Immanuel gasped and stepped forward.

"The most beautiful sight you will have ever seen," Immanuel said as the donkey nudged him in the back. "I offer myself to Papa all the time, and we speak face to face…offer yourself and see what happens," Immanuel said as I stared at the grass.

"I…" I stopped, mid-walk back to the kitchen. Our two shadows became one. "How do I submit?"

"My friend, that is a good question. Like this," Immanuel bowed slowly, not making eye contact.

"You've been doing that this whole time." I pushed him gently on the arm.

Maddie came and stood at the back glass door, and I lost my focus on Immanuel.

"Her journey is not like yours, but she already has met him. She yearns for more, my friend, and would walk beside you to meet the lion." Immanuel saw my face. I watched Maddie. "Something to think about," Immanuel brushed his donkey. "I will get the wine glasses ready and bake the bread. That is my specialty," Immanuel boasted. "Shall we?" he ushered me to the house.

Once inside, the smell of fresh food was overwhelming. I noticed from the back door that Mamaw had already gotten into the cheese and wine and was humming a tune that I could not recognize.

I lingered at the back door and tried to catch a glimpse of the lion.

"My friend," Immanuel brought me a glass of wine.

I looked him directly in the eyes. My Hispanic friend just smiled and went back to preparing the evening activities.

"Heaven calls this mercy," Immanuel suggested over his shoulder.

"Oh baby, Papa is coming," my Mamaw danced in the kitchen a little and then went back to stir something on the stove.

"Hey, you changed clothes," I said to Maddie, who had slipped on a yellow dress. "You look incredible." I knew my jaw had dropped a little. Maddie passively strutted for me, looking back. My heart felt warm around her.

"And took a shower upstairs, maybe even used your towel," Maddie whispered and winked.

"That's ok, just as long as you did not use my toothbrush," I grinned.

"John, you are being awfully quiet. What's on your mind?" Mamaw ate a piece of cheese and bread.

I just knew Papa, the great lion was on his way. I could see it in my mind, him walking towards the house. I recall that I was becoming quieter as the night went on; I slowed my wine consumption.

"I am getting focused on what is approaching the house right now," I said. Immanuel brought me a piece of bread and refilled my glass.

"For the body that was broken and for the blood that was spilled," I said. The kitchen of people watched me take communion.

Papa called with a soft roar just outside the gate.

"It is time," Immanuel said.

Maddie ran to look out the back door. The night lights illuminated the beast's eyes. The lion trotted quickly to meet Santo at the gate, waiting. The barks of a dog were satisfied with the calls from a lion, soft grunts of companionship.

"I almost want to cry. I am feeling something in me." I handed my glass of wine to Maddie, who took a sip, I grabbed her hand. "Mamaw likes coffee every evening at about three o'clock." Maddie winked at me and pushed me towards the lion.

The gate was not a hindrance for Papa, who jumped over quickly as Santo began to lick him in the face, wagging his tail, and rolled over in front of him, submitting. Papa swatted at Santo playfully with a mighty right hand. Santo got up, barked, and ran as Papa gave chase in play. Like two friends, the dog and lion played for several minutes as we watched from the back door.

Papa caught Santo after tripping the dog, and the two were rolling around on the grass, smashing a few flowers along the way. When the eyes of the lion met mine, playtime was over for dog and beast. Santo did not want to quit, and he immediately sat down in front of the lion and begged for more time. The growl of Papa signaled that playtime was over. The lion was here for me.

"Do I need my rifle?" I looked at Immanuel.

"No, my friend, just yourself. All of your food will be provided." Immanuel walked out the back door as I followed.

"He is magnificent." Maddie held my glass in her yellow sunflower dress.

"You wouldn't believe what his kindness looks like," Immanuel laughed as I choked on my own tears.

The lion had walked closer to the concrete patio and sat down in the green grass. Santo was next to him, his tail wagging continuously.

The lion was waiting for Immanuel's feet to touch the grass as he sprang forward to rub his powerful body on his son, who gave him love and affection back. The lion purred loudly and pushed Immanuel around with his massive head. Immanuel whispered to his Papa in a secret language.

I stood and waited on the concrete patio of the back porch, just waiting as Maddie and Mamaw watched from the open back door.

"Papa, take care of my boy," my Mamaw said and squeezed past Maddie, who followed her out the door and stood beside me.

The purrs of the lion rattled the wood roof above my head as Immanuel spoke with his arm around the lion.

"John, come forth and meet him. Papa needs you to meet him halfway."

Immanuel was right. As soon as my foot touched the grass, the lion's attention was on me entirely. Immanuel stepped back to avoid distraction and walked toward the gate he fixed, leaving me with Papa.

In all of its power, the lion turned toward the gate, stopped, and waited for me to follow him. Santo wanted to go. Papa nipped at him to stop him. The dog put his head down and went to his doghouse.

I cautiously followed the lion at a distance and looked back at Maddie, who waved at me.

"I will help around the farm, do not worry about this place." She smiled.

As Papa walked through the open gate before me, Immanuel petted him just for the moment.

"John, you can't learn anything, Señor, walking behind him," he encouraged me.

"Burn me, eat me," I said again. "I am trusting."

"Trust is important, my friend." Immanuel shut the gate behind us. Papa stopped so I could catch up. I noticed and hesitated. "You are in the wild now. There are secrets that Papa wants to tell you; let Him teach you." Immanuel latched the gate and turned to go back inside to finish out the night.

The lion and I stood illuminated by the moon and the stars.

"Now what?"

The lion took a few steps toward me, circled me, and finally nudged me with his head to move forward with him. I grabbed his mane gently as we walked side by side in the evening light. The grass became tall, but there was a visible trail to follow.

A pack of wolves began to howl in unison.

"Sounds like a war party," I said out loud. "A gun would be nice," I added, flicking my trigger finger in anticipation. Papa became angry at the challenge in the distance. He grabbed a bush with his mighty jaws ripping root and all out of the ground and flung the shrub through the night air. Papa paced back and forth, calling for a challenger to come along. A deep moan claimed his territory. On the other hand, I had taken a few steps back and found a stick to club a wolf with.

Papa scratched the earth with his back feet, relaxed, and urinated on the ground. I could see him panting in the darkness of night. He looked back to check on me. The mighty lion rubbed his body against mine. I petted him vigorously, scratching under his neck. He bumped into me, nudging me with his head, even nipping at my legs playfully.

I could barely see the light of the house. Leaving the familiar I followed Papa into the unknown. I submitted myself for a time. The lion would walk beside me for the remainder of the night—what seemed like all night—gaining my trust. Deep down, I believed he longed for this day just as I.

I was tired as Papa led me away from my everyday routines of life. I passed the thicket as fireflies illuminated the den of a king. He briefly waited and then grunted.

"Ok," was all I said as I continued to follow Him into the blackness. While walking with Him, the feeling I had was almost impossible to explain. The dew brushed my legs from the grass, but I never got wet.

We walked for what seemed like half the night. The tall grass opened up to a river. Someone had prepared a meal. A type of poultry roasted over the fire, an abundant supply of fruit, and of course wine and water to drink, I just stared at the wonder.

"This is a meal for a king." I stepped closer to the fire and feasted.

The poultry was quail that fell apart in my hands and melted in my mouth. The fruit was mango and honey that was prepared.

"Are you going to eat anything?" I leaned against a rock and enjoyed my meal. Papa just watched me as the fire reflected in his eyes. "I have a lot of questions."

Papa was quiet and even looked past me. He cleared his throat.

The sounds of the wolves howling just past our camp took his attention quickly. He rose to his feet with confidence and haste, jumped on the tallest rock at our campsite, and let out a roar that shook the ground. Silence set in as the howling was a little further away but not finished. Papa turned to check on me before he leaped into the tall grass and disappeared.

I sat alone for what seemed like an hour, eating my meal, tasting everything. The quail was something I had never tried; the feast was spectacular.

I turned to my right to see a Papa, holding a dead wolf in his mouth. The lion slammed the wolf down and ripped it apart right before my eyes. In the light of the moon and stars, I could still see him devouring the animal, crushing bone, and separating skin from the flesh.

"I am glad I just ate," I said as the sight was not the prettiest thing to watch. Papa ate until he was satisfied, walked over to a nearby bush, marked his territory, and returned to camp.

He was entertaining me as I drank his wine. I laughed at what looked like a frog darting to and fro, causing this great beast to search playfully. The lion slapped the grass with his mighty paws to jump back and prepare for another ambush. It seemed nothing that stood in his way was safe from attack.

"What did you bring me out here for?" I asked the lion, who decided to roll in the grass to scratch his own back. "Why am I here?" I hoped the lion would speak somehow to me. The lion laid down just on the other side of the fire, then licked himself a few times, only to stare at me, almost like he was waiting on something. His mighty eyes glistened under the stars like two burning candles.

"Where is your father?" I heard a soft voice say, like the wind blowing around the night air, the dust stirred around me, the grass bowed low in submission. I closed my eyes and shook my head. I had no reply and set my wine glass down to engage.

Until now, things had been so different.

"Did you bring me out here to ask me a question that would make me angry? Where is my father?" I raised my voice. The lion slapped his paw on the ground, roaring to get control of my emotions, and I quickly calmed down, easing back on my dirt mound as the calmness of the night returned. The lion grunted softly.

"I have no father," I said, pulling the grass by the roots and tearing up as the lion was getting up and walked over to me, my heart beating fast, not knowing if he was going to kill me. His paws were the size of my head, but he made no sound when they touched the ground.

Papa gently nudged my head with his, purring loudly. He laid down beside me, nipping at my legs. He could feel my nervousness, not adjusting quickly to this.

"Papa," I said, as his eyes met mine. "Why am I here?"

The lion stood quickly to his feet and ran past me with a gentle nudge, and half the night, we chased each other like little children in the tall grass just beside the Red River. I know now why Santo was always happy to see Papa. Under the pale moonlight hiding in the brush and grass, he would hide and wait for me to find him. I could barely see, but I searched for Papa, trailing him, but always the lion found me. Knocking me over to lay on me and rub me with his mighty head, his mane was like fire. I did not know it then, but he was claiming me as his own, over and over. The more I looked for him, the more he claimed me.

"Is this mercy?" I said while roughhousing in the open field. "To come down and search me out like you did, a lion calling from a thicket?" I asked while we both panted in the midnight air? The lion never spoke, but I could almost see a smile.

"Hey," I said. Papa turned his mighty head. It shifted the moon. "I know you can talk," I said, confidently. Papa answered by grunting, then calling out loud, stretching his neck to the fullest. "Secrets, so the kingdom of Heaven has secrets." I wanted in.

"I am going to prove myself to you that I can be trusted," I vowed. Papa continued to groom himself but stopped long enough for us to trade a look of trust as the stars submitted and the moonlight danced upon the river. I was alone with a lion and with no weapon, and I had found the peace that my soul longed for, and I was alone with God.

CHAPTER 11

When I awoke, there was something on my mind immediately trying to steal my peace. I sat, fidgeting.

"Papa, I need to tell you something. My contract is still open." I tossed a stick into the grass blindly. The lion stretched himself, yawning, presenting the world with a powerful jaw and teeth. "Lycan. I fear he will come after me and harm the ones who are important to me. I am pretty sure there is a price on my head, but maybe not." Since I arrived at the farm, I had kept this concern hidden from many. I thought of the farm with Mamaw and Maddie as the most essential things in my life.

The lion shook his mighty mane, swatting at a wasp that flew by. His behavior at times seemed careless, but if he was the image of God's power and mercy, he had authority over all, even the things that could hurt a man.

The fire burned slowly, with fresh-baked pastries, coffee, and a fruit arrangement.

"Are you going to join me?" I asked, surrendering to the opportunity to be with him.

The lion turned and came closer to the fire only to sit beside me, rolling over, almost causing me to spill my coffee.

"Immanuel knows something," I said.

Papa sat up in attention and gazed deeply into my eyes from several feet away.

I sensed that he was trying to tell me something, but for a moment I didn't want to hear it. At last, I sighed and accepted what the lion had been urging me to acknowledge.

"Is it about Lycan?" I asked, almost afraid to get the confirmation I was dreading.

I looked away briefly, but Papa kept his eyes on me and I finally looked back. "I do not want to go back to my old life." I wondered about the river to my right, and how its course changed after a significant flood, the lion patiently waited. I knew in my heart that he was prompting me to get my fears off my chest.

"Lycan is my equal in talent. He will more than likely have people with him trying to hunt me down, a team of paid killers," I said, pulling up some random pieces of grass and fighting a knot in my stomach. I knew what Lycan and his team were capable of doing. "If they come after me, I would have to kill them all. No mercy. It's not just about protecting myself, it's about protecting everyone I love."

When our eyes met again, all of my fear that was rising just vanished. I just knew, deep within, that if my past came back to hurt or even haunt me, Papa would be there to help me. I did not know how he would help, but the great lion would be there. My wandering mind began to settle by letting out a sigh of relief.

Papa turned quickly towards the tall grass, scanned the horizon by changing his posture, and I saw a wild boar on the edge of a tree line a distance of one hundred yards or so. The lion was on the hunt and was gone, not even making a sound, disappearing into the wall of grass.

I sat still leaning on the rock I slept close to last night, and all was quiet. The thoughts of Lycan disappeared, and I no longer worried about something I had no control over. I was alone with a providence from heaven, surrounded by food and the wild.

"Just leaning on a rock, eating breakfast, drinking coffee, waiting on God to get back," I said, reaching my hand out to get something delicious. The simplicity of the day's events seemed laughable.

I heard a noise coming from the river. I turned to see Immanuel in a boat, the splash of the net I will never forget.

"Did you make breakfast?" I asked, just wondering how all this was happening.

"Yeah, how was it?" Immanuel responded, smiling.

"I have been around the world, and nothing I have ever eaten compares to that!" I emphasized my fullness, even rubbing my belly just a little from the bank of the river.

"You will see me here and there, mostly it is about you and him." Immanuel pointed to the lion lying in the grass, watching from a short distance from me.

"Papa is back already?" I asked, looking over my shoulder as the lion returned to watch us.

"Papa is jealous right now, my friend," Immanuel said. The lion rolled over on his side and moaned in discontent as the two of us laughed and continued to converse.

"What are you doing now, besides just fishing?" I asked, curious.

"Just preparing lunch while you go have a walk with Papa in a bit," Immanuel said, tossing the net into the shallow end of the river. He retrieved some fish and placed them in a basket. "When I see Maddie, my friend, is there anything you want me to ask her?" Immanuel continued to prepare his net to be tossed into the water.

A thought ran through my mind of her, our conversations together, and how she looked in that dress.

"I have something to ask her myself, but I just need a little courage," I added.

"You already know she is gonna say yes, my friend," he said, focusing on the net, and dropping a few fish in a basket again.

"Would you like to try?" he offered, holding up the net.

"Yes!" I said while running to get into the boat.

"I can get closer," he suggested, holding his hand up to stop me, but I was already hip-deep in the water, and reaching out, he grabbed me with one hand and with ease set me securely in the boat with him.

"A little water never hurt anybody," I added. I made sure that Papa was okay with this, he replied with a groan and laid down hard again in the grass, scratching his back.

"He is excited about you taking a walk with him in a bit but still a little jealous."

"How jealous?" I asked, curious.

Immanuel's eyes locked onto Papa's in a loving connection. "I would say maybe 5 minutes, and he is going to do something to get you on the bank with him," Immanuel said, laughing gently.

"Let me show you how to do that," I said, taking the net from Immanuel, trying to mimic his actions from earlier only to have the net wrapped around myself; I would have to admit he was patient. "I got it. Wait, no, I had it." I turned this way and then that way, one foot was in the boat, and the other was out. I tripped over the basket of fish. "You would think I could walk better than this," I said, laughing. "Sorry about the fish." Immanuel motioned to not worry about the fish as he picked up my mess. "Ok, so I hold this part of the net like so, and then…."

"Just throw the net into the deep. There is more grace there," he said. "Do not worry about form. This is your first time, Señor." Immanuel said as I paused.

"Everything here at the farm has been a lesson. Is this a lesson?" I asked, holding the net, like a spring ready to be sprung. "I am not afraid to take a risk," I said, fixing to heave that net with all my might, swinging my hips.

"Should have no problem asking Maddie to marry you," Immanuel said.

"Jesus!" I said, losing my balance as the net weights sent me falling headfirst into the water. I grabbed the tail rope as the net went straight down. I was holding on by a few fingers, feeling more embarrassed than anything.

"Immanuel," I said. He calmly walked out of the boat and came to my rescue, holding out his hand and smiling the whole time. I grabbed it, and once again, he picked me up as if I was nothing to set my feet on the side of the boat. He collected the net while still standing on the water as my clothes were dripping continuously. "How deep is it here, and what are you preparing me for?" I asked, taking a breath of air.

"What do you think, my friend?"

I sat there for just a minute wanting to say something out loud that had been on my heart ever since I saw her in that yellow dress at Mamaw's house. "I am not afraid of any man," I said, placing a single fish back in the basket. "But the thought of asking Maddie on a date is terrifying."

"We think it is a great idea," Immanuel said, setting the net down in the boat. "What did you learn from throwing the net just then, Señor?" He said. "Think about how this relates to you and Maddie. The first time, deep water, a helping hand if you fail." He spoke just a little slower.

"That I am taking the biggest risk of my life, and if I fail, you will be there to pick me back up." I knew that I loved her.

Immanuel's expression was like the sun. "If we were with you at your birth, why would we turn our back on you when you needed it the most?" He again smiled.

My eyes filled with tears.

"We have about two minutes before Papa swims out here to get you, my friend." The lion had come to the edge of the water and sat staring and chuffed loudly.

"Have you broken bread and poured wine for people who did not want to eat or drink?" I asked. Immanuel's expression changed, he wept softly and turned his face. He stood on the boat preparing his net to cast, taking his time to answer my question.

"We offer even though we will be rejected. As it is in heaven, we hope that it will be on earth." He said, wiping his face. "Hope is powerful...Papa wants you now."

I stood to my feet, looking for a place to jump in. "You never answered how deep it was!" I said, facing my body towards Papa but looking back to Immanuel.

"Señor, if you let me get closer to the bank, you can..."

I dove in the water and swam the remaining fifteen yards or so to the bank to get to Papa. The lion met me, even nudging me with his body as I stepped onto the muddy bank.

"Hold on." I was trying to stand. He pulled my clothes gently with his teeth. When I finally got to a walk, he continually rubbed his body on me until I stopped to pet him and return the affection.

"I told you we have waited for this day for a long time," Immanuel hollered from the boat. I waved before chasing Papa into the tall grass.

CHAPTER 12

"Wait, just hold it right there," Paul said as the smell of urine from the nursing home came back faintly and he tried to make sense of this old warrior's story. Paul leaned back in his seat, rubbing his face and eyes, almost smiling. He could hear laughter from the room next to them. "So, all of what you told me is true?" Nothing of what Paul learned from his childhood studies about God would declare this valid.

John smiled, exposing wrinkles and age. "Every bit of this story is true!" He breathed deeply, taking a quick gaze out past the bushes, and he softly spoke. "Such a beautiful invitation."

"To be eaten by a lion!" Paul snickered.

"What do you have to lose?" John replied, turning towards Paul. His response was enough for him to be quiet for just a moment. His words struck a nerve.

"So why do you sneak around here marking people with sharpies if the killer in you is no longer a part of your life?" Paul asked.

"Like I said, I just get bored," John added with a bit of laughter. Paul paused in aggravation.

"So, if I do not chase the lion, life…" Paul waited.

The smile John had turned upside down. "Life will continue to become darker and darker. The answers you are seeking are out there." The old man turned and pointed to the hedgerows of tall bushes just on the property edge as the squeak of a rolling cart approached.

"Mr. Hunt, we noticed you were not at breakfast, so we brought you something." A heavy-set African American lady said. She was pretty in the face and carried kind eyes. "The new guy with big plans, I brought you something also." Paul smiled but was intrigued by how fast gossip traveled here. "Miss Davenport's refrigerator is not running."

John slapped Paul's leg with his unsteady hand, "You had better go check that out."

"Okay, I will tell Miss Davenport that you are on your way to check her out," the lady replied.

"Wait, what. I did not say that." Paul shifted in his seat as the lady winked at him and turned with her cart.

"What just happened?" Paul asked the old man.

"Sounds like you have a date." John smiled.

Paul shook his head and took a look at his brunch. Paul placed it on the floor in its foam container, having no appetite. John ate his sausage biscuit in a few bites.

"Coffee!" John said, giving Paul his cup to fill and pointed at the coffee maker just down the hall. Paul, out of respect, fulfilled this old man's request.

"Okay!" Paul said, even though he hesitated knowing that Miss Davenport could just pop out from behind something, and he would melt like butter. The last thing Paul wanted to face today was why he could not move on from his beloved Sara.

"Black, no sugar. Like my women!" the old man said with a giggle. Paul could still hear John tapping that window as if the lion was going to just jump out and take him on one last run in that thicket.

Paul passed several residents' rooms only to see them just staring at a television. The blinds were closed as some just sat on the edge of their beds, and their eyes met Paul's. He did not see hope in them. It was almost like looking into the mirror every morning for the last seven months.

One resident was sitting on the threshold of her room. Her wheel-chair touched the hallway. She was partly dressed, but it was the gnawing on a cigar that caused Paul to stop. She was a little thing, and she looked like something harmless.

"You look nice today." Paul rummaged in his pocket for one of the mints he had robbed from Terry's office. "Peppermint? It's sugar-free." Her slow gaze upwards to meet Paul's eyes should have warned him about her disposition.

"I'll show you where to put that peppermint! You Jackass!"

He laughed. He was a little confused but mostly shocked that some-one so tiny could produce such rage. He tried politely to step aside as her wheelchair ran over his toe. It was more like a pinch of pain, and just enough to make him regret that peppermint. "Bye," he said and hoped he had left on good terms.

The squeak of her wheelchair would warn the next room of the incoming rage of eighty-five pounds. "Jackass!" she yelled into the neigh-boring room, then she turned back to Paul and gave him the middle finger.

"Shame on you, Miss Lockey!" The LPN walking down the hall quickly turned her wheelchair to prevent her from flashing innocent pe-destrians. "That finger is not made for that."

Miss Lockey crossed her arms like a child who hadn't gotten her way and stuck her tongue out.

"So sorry, new guy." The nurse spoke to Paul before wheeling Miss Lockey toward the lobby. He turned to check on Mr. Hunt, who had found Paul's breakfast and began eating it. Paul laughed because his ap-petite was just coming back.

"Are you going to eat this?" John said with a mouth full of food as their eyes met.

"Go ahead, I'll be okay." Paul just waved as he committed to getting the coffee.

The coffee was fresh in the hallway. Paul did not notice the tempera-ture of the coffee and Miss Davenport sneaking up behind him.

"Hey, you!" she said.

The world turned black as he dumped his coffee on the floor, on the coffee maker, and on both hands, giving himself a good burn. The pain was pretty intense for about two seconds. He closed both eyes and bit his lip.

"It's okay," Paul said. "I have an extra layer of skin that just grows back." Paul tried not to run her off and seem vulnerable simultaneously. When he opened his eyes, Mrs. Davenport covered her face with paper forms.

"Do you call it miracle skin? It grows only when coffee is poured on it!" She broke the silence with her giggle. "You poor thing." That was all she said before assisting Paul in the clean-up process. "I need a janitor in the coffee maker hallway. The new guy made a mess," she spoke into her radio. She carried herself well and with confidence.

"Someone will clean this up. Let's just make sure the floor is dry and not a slip hazard." She wiped some coffee from his hands. Paul could hear John laughing down the hall. "So, some things we need to talk about. The first thing is, how is your first day? Second, when are you coming by to sign some papers? The third thing is, the administration department is going out for drinks tomorrow. Do you think you can make it? Meet the staff?"

Paul simply stared at her for what seemed to be several seconds. "I would like that."

"I think you are going to fit right in." She smiled.

"I look forward to fitting in." That was all he could say.

"What happened to your head?" She leaned closer.

Paul was not about to tell her of the lion in the thicket. "Something startled me yesterday, while I was…"

"Well, we meet at the Steakhouse over on Blanchard Street to drink wine and eat at seven. I will save you a seat next to me. Wear something nice, but casual. Here is my card, and text me when you are on your way!" she concluded by walking back towards her office but not before swatting Paul on the arm with those forms. "Come by later and fill out these forms."

Paul bit his lip as he watched her walk away.

"Coffee!" John said from down the hall. Paul shook his head and came back to reality. He held up the cup to let John see. The old man motioned Paul back with a light wave.

"Um, here you go!" Paul took his seat beside John, who seemed eager, and pulled on Paul's pants leg to sit down; or maybe he just wanted his coffee. Paul stared at the floor.

"My wife Sara died almost seven months ago," Paul blurted out his past to this old man in a nursing home.

John stopped immediately what he was doing. Paul never felt more naked than he did right at that moment. He buried his face in his hands, tried to hide his grief, then he just broke. A few residents looked up from their wheelchairs as John comforted Paul.

"There, there, you do not want to let the whole world know that you are a mess." John patted Paul on the arm in a comforting manner. "So, tell me about Sara, something that will make you laugh," John suggested.

Paul needed a minute to gain his composure. He looked around to make sure nobody had seen him cry. It was too late. A nurse had stopped working to look in his direction. John pointed to the water fountain behind Paul, who needed to wash his face. Paul gathered his composure at the water fountain. "How about the first time she farted in front of me," Paul said with a chuckle.

"Tell me." John took a sip of his coffee, allowing Paul to retake his seat.

"Um, we had just gotten back from our honeymoon. You know, eager to start a new life together, and while unpacking from our long trip in the living room, Sara just disappeared. I found her in the laundry room, hiding. When we saw each other, she blushed and ran past me like something was wrong; that was when the smell hit. It was terrible," Paul said as he started to laugh dramatically. "When I found her, she was in the bathroom with the door closed. Sara would not come out for almost an hour from embarrassment."

"How does that make you feel?" John laughed with Paul.

"Happy!" Paul replied quickly, wiping tears from his eyes. "She brought joy to my life."

"Good! Where did you propose to her at?" The old warrior wanted to talk more and his eyes gleamed.

"It was a vineyard in California. I was absolutely terrified out of my mind. I just kept telling myself I needed just a few seconds of courage to change my life." Paul smiled.

"What was she doing before you proposed?" John asked.

"Sara had walked a few feet away to pick up pieces of the vines that were trimmed and lying on the ground. When she turned around, there I was on one knee. We brought the vines home and planted them. I just cannot get those things to stay alive. They die every year." Paul chuckled and breathed a sigh of relief as his laughter came back down to ground zero, and they both sat quietly for a few moments. Paul thought about several things looking around the facility and wiped his face.

"If you leave now, you are going to miss the rest of the story!" John emphasized.

"Why would I leave?" Paul asked curiously.

John tapped the window as the black butterfly returned and perched on the window, gently moving his wings in the sun.

"Change is coming," John said as Paul looked past the insect and did not see anybody.

"Who?" Paul asked.

John tapped the window a little more aggressively, this time on the butterfly. "Change is coming very soon. My friend has been here all morning just spending time with me. That, to me, means one thing. Papa is coming to get me. That is why you need to hear the rest of the story." John sighed.

"Where is Papa going to take you?" Paul asked. "Into the thicket?"

"Home." That was all the old warrior said. "I am going home."

Paul shifted in his seat and adjusted Miss Davenport's business card in his pocket, the corners were jabbing his thigh. "I really want you to continue."

"The next time the lion appears, you had better chase Papa into that thicket," John said with his finger pointing at Paul. "You will regret it the rest of your life if you don't."

"I am tired of regret." Paul thought of his future. He was ready to leave the sadness.

John laughed. "Now, let's get back to the story."

CHAPTER 13

I chased Papa into the tall grass and, from there, we disappeared into the unknown. He was fast, and my lungs burned, but my energy and stamina seemed sustained. From time to time, Papa would look back to check on me, but his pace was consistent. He never seemed to grow faint or weary, like one who never slumbers or sleeps. I trusted him as I have never trusted anyone in my life. We crossed streams of water together, deep waters of crystal beauty. At times I could not touch the bottom as the waters slapped me in the face.

At other times we would pass through the terrain of what seemed like death. The forest burned, and the animals ran to-and-fro searching for safety. It was a time of feast and famine, it seemed. We would step into one extreme of the environment to experience the opposite.

We passed through a swamp. Mud was up to my thighs. Snakes laid on fallen trees in the dark waters; it was not pleasant as Papa's presence made the serpent slip off into the water. I kept my eyes on Papa, knowing that fear could easily cause me to stop my progress.

We stopped for a meal that was already prepared for us. There was a feast of fresh grilled fish, fresh bread, honey, and a jar. I knew Immanuel did this and searched for the set of footprints that I recognized in the dirt. His trail was easy to follow. I missed my companion.

Papa and I sat alone. He watched while I scarfed down my food. He scanned the horizon from time to time. Papa smelt the random air and closed his eyes. It was such a beautiful sight.

When I was finished eating, I had a pile of fish bones that I tossed into the fire to be consumed. I pushed the rocks together to put out the fire. Papa turned to face me when I grabbed the water jug, a piece of clay shaped into a jar and cool to the touch. He looked like something extraordinary was about to happen, his powerful face was highlighted and his eyes gleamed with pride.

I stopped to admire the writings on the jar because I noticed Papa.

"Love, joy, peace, kindness, goodness, patience, hope, and self-control. All of this in one jar?" I noticed a flower that was dried up just beside me on the ground that had turned brown, barely a leaf to show. "Here you go!" I gave it a little drink. The water covered the plant and watered the ground, holding the little plant up. Slowly, the plant became straight as flowers sprouted from the once lifeless plant. A beautiful white flower.

"Wow, what is in here?" I asked, smelling the container.

"Lily of the valley. One of my favorite flowers," Immanuel said from a few yards away, holding a walking staff. "Papa asked me to come back." He looked over at Papa in a respectful manner. "Just to explain something."

I politely smiled. "I always enjoy your company."

"Your heart is ready." Immanuel walked closer to talk.

I paused in the noon sun. Papa had now sat up.

"Ready for what?" I asked.

"To hear like we do, to see like we do, and to feel just like we do!" Immanuel emphasized kneeling down to get on my level. "To understand why this had to happen," he said, showing me the scars on his wrists. "You no longer possess nothing; you now have room in your heart for us."

I laughed as joy touched my heart and eyes. A black butterfly fluttered around me and eventually landed on my arm.

"I once was scared of you," I said, looking at the butterfly. "Just a crazy memory of me sitting in the grass. I had to be just barely a year old or so." I shook my head with an awkward laugh. "I remember feeling so alone."

"You associate the butterfly with despair and turmoil," Immanuel said, taking a more comfortable seat on the grass next to me. "We associate this one with change." He pointed to the black butterfly, slowly moving his wings in peace. "Change is good."

My heart began to ache, just a little.

"Just take a sip of this water, even with the pain of this butterfly, my friend."

I took one last look at the jar made from clay before taking a drink of the water Immanuel gave as the chills ran down my back and all over my body.

"Wow," I said as joy returned. The butterfly had no effect on my mood or physical being at the moment. "That is some good stuff."

"Drink the whole thing, Señor." Immanuel insisted. I did in one big gulp and placed the cup in his hands. "How do you feel?" he asked.

"Much different." I stood to my feet. I had thought of something unfamiliar and very uncomfortable in my eyes. I wanted to see my natural father and get closure to our relationship and let go. The black butterfly made me think of him, my last memory of us.

"So, we understand you want to see your father?" Immanuel called me out.

I hesitated but then spoke my heart. "Maybe if my dad meets you and Papa, his life will change also!" I said, selflessly.

Immanuel approached me and placed a hand on my shoulder. "Now you are thinking like we do, my friend. Papa already had something in mind." Immanuel bowed. "I will have food ready at your next stop, but Papa wants to have that moment with you."

I gave Immanuel a funny look.

"Is he still alive, my father?" I asked.

"He wishes things were different, but he has no idea of where or who you are," Immanuel said.

"I promise I will not kill him. And what is in that water?" I laughed.

"That water is made from sacrifice." Immanuel bowed and stepped aside as Papa called to me.

I stood in front of the lion, who gave me a half-hearted smile.

"I know you can talk," I said as he turned and began his majestic trot as I followed. Follow I did. For what seemed like another day, we ran together. This time it was day and night without stopping. I never became hungry or tired. We did not stop to eat or sleep. The weather seemed to change like the terrain.

I could tell by the sun that we were headed on a northern path. My guess was probably mid-Arkansas or Oklahoma. After over sixteen hours of running, Papa began to trot. The sun was quickly fading behind the trees as darkness approached. I wondered if we would sleep under that bridge we were headed toward.

"How far did we run?" I asked Papa, who did not respond. "I am going to get you to say something before I die."

There was a glow coming from the bottom of that bridge, a fire. A barbed-wire fence separated us from the bridge now. I could see it in the twilight of the dark.

"What now?" I asked the lion.

Papa turned toward me and rubbed his head and body around me, almost circling me. I returned the affection with a hug. When his eyes met mine, I knew I had to cross that barbed wire fence alone and find out what was under that bridge. A basket of food hung on a post, I noticed.

"I understand." I climbed over the fence and reached back to get the basket. Food was always an invitation to something around there. I did not take my time, for the grass between the bridge and I was wet and cold. I was doing this alone as a cold air chill hurried me to find warmth.

"Who goes there?" a voice spoke out as the fire presented a shadow of a man.

"John," I said. "I have food."

"I could use something to eat," a man replied without any hesitation and stepped forward where we could see each other. "Do I know you?" The man asked.

"I don't know, but we could share a meal." I held the basket like a peace agreement. The man was big, almost replicating me, but older. He wore an old jacket that was torn, his pants needed to be washed, and he looked dirty.

"The church down the road will stop and bring me food sometimes. Are you with them?" he asked as I stood just outside his campsite under the bridge.

"No, I was just running with..."

"Running at night?" He asked while sitting back down by his fire and adding some wood. "Come and have a seat if you like. Everybody is running from something."

I took his offer and sat on a rock just big enough for me, and began to look through the basket of food as my appetite had come back with a vengeance. I looked back toward the lion in the darkness but I could not see him.

"What did you bring me?" the man asked, shuffling some things around before violently coughing. "God help me," he said while spitting a mouth full of blood to the ground beside me. "I have to lay off the cigarettes."

My eyes said it all as he finally caught his breath and rested. "Sandwich?" I held out several. Not knowing what they were, he grabbed them with both hands.

"Thanks." That was all he replied, nestling back into his seat.

"Egg salad. One of my favorite sandwiches," I said.

"Cool, mine too." He began to enjoy his meal. "So, what is your name?" he asked.

"John Hunt," I said, not hardly making eye contact at first. The sound of crackling wood and flames became deafening.

"Hunt?" he asked.

"Yeah, I haven't seen my dad since I was tiny." We made eye contact.

"Well, I had a son with that name," he said.

"Then what?" I replied quickly. I wanted answers and dismissed his feelings. "What happened to Mom? Why did you leave me?" His eyes widened as the tension was evident.

"How can this be?" He sat his sandwich down and wiped tears from his eyes. I stared at him, waiting for his response. I was not angry like I thought I would be. I felt pity as I produced a thermos of coffee and two cups. I poured him a cup of coffee as he cried, hiding his face. He took the cup from me with a hand on his shoulder, and I took my seat.

I told him my life story, what happened to me after he left me, the struggles I had in my teen years, and my life as a murderer for hire. I told him all about Immanuel, the farm, and the lion. Also, how badly I wanted to kill him until I came to stay at the farm. He listened with intensity, and he fought tears and rounds of coughing.

"Your mother died of an overdose. She had a secret addiction that I did not know about." That was all he said about her. "I just gave up on life and you at the same time," he said. I wanted to ask more questions, but it would have only stirred strife within each other. I wanted to move on past him, the mistakes he made.

We finished the sandwiches as the fire gave us warmth.

"So, you're not mad at me?" he asked.

"No, I moved on past this," I said quickly.

"You're not going to kill me?" he asked, half-jokingly.

"No, that wouldn't do any good for anybody."

"Excuse me, Señors, may I?" The one who loved me as a brother stepped into the light of the fire holding a bottle of wine and bread. I knew what he was here to do.

"Do I need to leave?" I asked.

"John, Papa is waiting for you." Immanuel extended a hand toward my dad. "Your dad is about to take a journey with us. I have made a special place just for him. A place of no more bridges." Immanuel smiled.

My dad coughs violently again, spitting out blood. "I hope it's to a shelter or hospital." He laughed.

The lion roared in the darkness. "Dad, I have to go. I'll see you later," I said, getting up from my rock and making my way into the darkness, ready to trust the lion again.

"Good to see you, John," he replied.

I stopped just outside the camp and listened.

"For a body that was broken…" I heard Immanuel say as I made my way back to Papa and crossed the fence. The lion was there waiting.

"My dad is about to die? Isn't he?"

Papa placed his head in my arms and chuffed softly. I looked back one last time to see my dad take a drink of the wine that Immanuel gave him as I wept. I was grateful for the journey he was about to take. It was a beautiful invitation.

CHAPTER 14

When I awoke the next morning, I was in our original camping spot just beside the river. As usual, the fire was going and the sunrise was breathtaking. I was alone at the site, and food was prepared neatly—fruits, honey, coffee, and bread. A few eggs still in the shell waited to be cracked and cooked. They welcomed me as I poured the morning coffee.

I stood up to get a good look around as Immanuel and Papa were in the boat together a short distance from the bank where I was. Just far enough to where I could not understand what Immanuel was saying. Papa listened. At several different times in their conversing, the two would place their heads together in unity. I admired from the shore for a short while.

I returned to my seat and started breakfast, keeping a watchful eye on them as they spent time together. I enjoyed my meal, even sitting back down and waiting patiently, drinking the morning coffee as I heard the paddles from the boat begin to strike the water. I quickly got up from my seat and went and stood on the bank of the river as the lion claimed the front of the boat while Immanuel paddled.

"I was wondering what happened to you all," I said, as Papa jumped from the boat and walked briefly in the water to return to shore.

"Just a little talk," Immanuel said.

"So, I saw my dad drink the wine and eat the bread. Is he going to chase the lion into the thicket?"

"No, my friend." Immanuel hesitated and looked at Papa and paused. I, too, turned to look at Papa, also hoping they would clue me in on my father's journey. "He is coming to stay with us forever," Immanuel said as he turned to push the boat back into the water using his paddle.

"Wait, where are you going?" I asked.

"I need to be alone, my friend," Immanuel said.

I politely pushed the boat off the bank in assistance. "I figured you would be happy about my dad," I said still holding on to the boat as Immanuel did not say anything at first.

"Let me go Señor." Immanuel was clearly bothered, even grabbing a paddle to push himself away as I held onto the boat, wanting answers. "Let me go," he said slowly, with intensity.

I did, finally. I let him go and he turned the boat around and aggressively paddled into the river, a place where I could not follow.

"John!" Immanuel said.

"Yes," I replied, hoping for another fishing lesson.

"There is one in the group that took the bread and wine from me. His name is Henry and, like you, he hated his life and wants something new!" Immanuel said from the boat.

I thought for a second.

"I do not know of a Henry," I replied.

"Show him mercy, like Papa showed you mercy! Papa wants to spend time with him." Immanuel turned and paddled away and I watched him leave.

"Is Lycan coming for me?" I asked, with no response. I turned to Papa and repeated myself only to turn and watch my friend paddle away. The lion came and stood beside me on the bank and that was all he did. I knew that my time with the lion in the thicket was coming to an end.

"I think it is time we head back to the farm." I wanted to see Maddie. The lion nudged me with his head, nipped at my side, and turned and ran at a pace that I could keep up with. "Not so fast, I just ate," I argued, but he never slowed down. From there, we ran several hours until I could see the top of the chimney from my Mamaw's house, passing the dark thicket where Papa and I had our first meeting, a place of remembrance for me.

A heaviness began to weigh me down as I was getting fatigued from running. For the first time in several days, I could feel my lungs burning. The strength that I had flowing through my veins these last several days had faded fast. The sweat poured from my head and my body began to ache and cramp. The realities of human life hit me hard as I craved water.

"What happened?" I asked Papa as the lion slowed down and marked his territory claiming this land as his. "I thirst for the first time in several days," I said, rubbing my aching muscles that had been stressed. The cold air hurt, and my tongue kept sticking to the top of my mouth. I yawned and wanted to lay down in the grass to sleep. Papa continued and walked toward the edge of the property as Santo began to bark from a short distance that I could not see.

The smoke from the chimney never looked so good and I wanted to lay down and sleep for several days as exhaustion hit me hard. The dew saturated my shoes and pants. I felt the cold like I did when I had a talk with my father under that bridge.

"John." I heard a familiar voice.

"Mamaw," I said, as I finished walking the rest of the trail and rounded that corner.

"Maddie! John is home!" she said, as I made it to the gate and turned to not see Papa behind me; his tail was all that I saw disappearing into the tall grass. I waited for a few minutes as the sound of people's feet came toward me. I hoped Papa would return soon.

"Where is the lion?" Maddie asked, causing me to forget about Papa and turn to give my friend all the attention she deserved.

"He was just here," I said, looking into her eyes and giving a half-hearted attempt to point behind me, where the lion once stood. "Wow, I missed you." I leaned on the gate Immanuel built.

"Well, a girl like me is hard to come by," Maddie said, letting her hair fall just right.

"Papa and Immanuel are very fond of you. I can see why." I kicked the grass under my feet as Maddie waited for me to ask the question she longed for. My heart was in my throat but it never felt more right than now.

"I think I will go inside and prepare something to eat," my Mamaw said, rubbing her hands together and clapping softly.

"So, how about you and me, just get away from the farm?" It was all I could come up with to say.

"Do you mean like a date? That sounds like fun!" She paused and made herself clear. "Sure!" Maddie laughed. "I thought you were going to ask me something stupid like do I like beef hash or something?"

"No, that would be so not cool." I scratched my head because I started thinking about beef hash just a few minutes ago. I was so hungry.

"Sandwiches are ready and on the back porch!" Mamaw said, as I entered the backyard, closed the gate, and gave Maddie the hug she deserved, sending chills up and down my body.

"Baby, you are going to sleep well tonight," Mamaw said as I gave her a hug too.

"I am happy to be home but I already want to go back out there," I said, pointing toward the back of the property, toward the thicket.

"Santo!" I said as that Cur dog was so happy to see me, he licked my face and hands, then smelled my pants really good, only to run back to the gate to sit and wait for Papa.

"That dog spends half the day just sitting, waiting on Papa to come and get him. Just complete and total surrender," she said, as I too could feel that aching in my heart again for the lion to come back for me. "John, go in the kitchen and wash up first," she said, as walked past the food on the back porch and directly into the kitchen, where Maddie followed.

That smell of fresh bread and wine, I will never forget. "I could just stay in here all day," Maddie said as I agreed. "Just something about this place."

"God dwells here," I said as I washed the dirt from my hands.

"That is the only way to explain!" Maddie concluded.

"Imagine trying to explain to the world what I have experienced?" I looked out the window and then turned to face Maddie, who took a step toward me.

"I would sure try, every time that I could. I would tell your story." Maddie was prettier than ever. She picked some flowers before she came inside the house and held them like a bride on her wedding day. Maddie had chosen me like I had chosen her.

Right there in that kitchen, I kissed her.

CHAPTER 15

I tried to sleep that night, but the noise I heard from outside caused me to explode out of bed early, almost 4:00 am. I grabbed the M1 from over the fireplace and searched for why Santo had barked suddenly. I opened the back door and was greeted by my friend. After a scratch on the ear, he returned to where he came from in the dark. The concrete on the back porch was cold, and the autumn weather was welcomed. Santo would give bark, whine, and bark again. Then a pause followed by a distant roar from the lion in the thicket. I took a seat and listened to the two converse back and forth for several minutes. It was a beautiful invitation.

After a few minutes, my anxiety had disappeared, and I decided to go ahead and get up early and return to my room to get dressed and start the coffee pot. I clutched my M1 like it was a part of me. I knew Papa would be with me, but I assumed I was being warned for a reason and took it to heart. I returned to my seat on the back porch. The brisk air stirred me as I laid my rifle on the table and enjoyed my morning. The rising sun had not begun to come up over the trees or hint of the day's awakening when the back door slid open.

"Baby, you're up early," my Mamaw said, cradling her cup of coffee. "It is too dark out here. I got to have me some light." Her arm reached for the patio light switch...

"No light," I said as she stopped and came back to sit beside me. "The light illuminates us as we sit here."

My Mamaw stared at my rifle in the dark of the early morning. "John, did Papa say something to upset you?" she asked.

"Nothing like that." I waved my hand in protest.

"So, why are you carrying around your rifle again? Sitting in the dark?" she asked, smiling at me but with concern in her voice.

"Immanuel was upset, distraught actually just before I came back. I have never seen him upset," I said.

"He gets like that when someone does not accept his bread and his wine. He has to go off alone in the wilderness. I think that is when Papa and Immanuel have some of their best conversations." She smiled, taking a polite sip of her coffee. "His heart hurts."

The conversation made me think of my dad. "Oh, Papa took me to make peace with my dad. He ate the bread and drank the wine," I added.

"Your father? You met your father?" she asked.

"Yeah. He is going home to stay with Papa and Immanuel, a special place prepared just for him," I said with a tear in my eye as my Mamaw had tears rolling down her face.

"That is such good news! I prayed for him for years."

"I told him everything, where I had been. He was obviously sick, and I knew that mercy had found him when Immanuel showed up with bread and wine." I noticed a reflection coming from the garage door by the shop, something shiny. After I adjusted my eyes, I said, "You went and bought a truck."

"I always wanted a blue truck! Oh, and the bullets for your gun should be on the front porch this morning. I found a great deal for a thousand rounds, and you got extra clips and a pouch to carry everything."

"What made you do that while I was gone?" I asked, knowing that I needed more ammo.

"I heard Papa tell me that you needed more bullets for that gun while you were out there chasing him in that thicket. I just did like I was told." Her little chubby cheeks produced a satisfied grin as I gave her a kiss and returned to my seat. The M1 still lay on the table.

"So, I guess it is time I just tell you what I used to do for a living. No secrets," I said.

"Wait, our coffee cup is not full, it's getting cold," she said. I patiently waited in the dark as she brought coffee and filled our coffee cups before I began. She returned to her seat, bright-eyed and bushy-tailed.

"Let's see, been a while." I scratched my head thinking about telling this part of my life. "I joined the military at eighteen. I had to, or go to jail. I really liked to fight and steal, and I was good at both of those." I thought briefly. "I went to war, killed some people." I checked on Mamaw, whose eyes were wide and expressive. "I figured if I was good at killing people, why not get paid to do so. I didn't mind it at the time." Mamaw was doing fine, but she had stopped drinking her coffee and was just staring at me.

"Then what?" she asked as she had gotten up and moved Immanuel's tool belt and hung it on a nail.

"I was planning on getting out, and I said it plenty of times that the military doesn't pay me enough to kill people. I guess word got to the right people that I wanted to make money, killing people." I thought for a minute. "Are you okay over there?"

"Fine, fine!" she said with wide eyes. "So you were a hired murderer?"

"Basically. The people that I killed were in drug cartels or child molesters. It is still murder, no matter what. I took away their chance to chase Papa, to have bread and wine with Immanuel. I did that." I paused briefly. "I was selfish. I showed them no mercy, and instead, I received mercy by coming back to a farm. I realized just how small I was when I came here." I smiled at Mamaw. "I am not the same person I was only a few months ago."

"Papa changed you, didn't he?" she asked.

"My world got smaller, and I made room for Papa," I said.

Mamaw looked towards my rifle. "Are one of those bad guys coming for you?" she asked kindly.

"Yes, I think so. My last contract is still open," I said. "I was set up, and they were waiting on me. Betrayed by an inner circle of wealthy people who made the call. Lycan was brought in to make me disappear. He is also a hired murderer. He was the only other contract killer that I feared. He's a monster." I sat up in my seat, slowly looking around. "Did you hear that? Papa is coming," I said as the wind spoke to me.

"When?" she asked.

"Soon, maybe after breakfast."

"Well, I will get started on that while you are drinking your coffee. No need to chase Papa on an empty stomach."

I soon followed because my stomach was growling. I returned my rifle over the fireplace where I kept it. I took my seat on the barstool and started on my third cup of coffee as Mamaw wanted to know the update with Maddie in detail. I took the time and filled her in on what Immanuel told me on the boat, while she started breakfast. Then I detailed the lion as best as possible in the thicket, some parts I kept to myself. Within a few minutes, she placed a food platter on the bar. Of course, I had to slide some pies out of the way to make room for breakfast.

"Just a quick meal," she said as if it was nothing to make eggs, bacon, toast, and oatmeal while having a detailed conversation with me all in under ten minutes.

"Maddie has some big shoes to fill," I said and reached for my fork. I stopped briefly and remembered how hungry and weak I became as I returned here after spending time with the lion in the thicket. I even remembered feeling that way mildly when I talked to my dad, tired and hungry. I gave my Mamaw a wandering look while I prepared to eat my breakfast and asked her about it. "Why did I not hunger or thirst while I ran with the lion?"

"John, your flesh was suppressed while you ran with Papa. He did that so your soul and his spirit could commune. Eventually, all that you held deep within was dealt with, and you were healed of much of your trauma. That is why you never felt hunger, but you enjoyed everything to the fullest. Your flesh which will get tired and hungry, became more active as you returned here because we used it every day. Your flesh basically tells you that it's time to eat, sleep, and do other stimulating stuff. Also, when you met your dad, you were in the flesh, so you could practice love as an everyday person. You forgave your dad and let go of much. You let a good time be placed within your soul also above else. You had closure."

"I have closure now. So that is what it feels like," I said.

"That is why it was easier for you to come back after you ran with Papa and asked Maddie out on a date," she smiled. "You can now go and start your family, and you will not fail as your father did."

"Wow." That is all I said. I heard the gate open from the outside, and the animals began to make their welcomed sounds.

"Immanuel is here." My Mamaw was looking out the kitchen window. I finished my coffee, took the last bit of breakfast and devoured it and kissed her on the cheek, and went upstairs to get ready to go outside.

I returned to see how my friend was doing. I opened the back door while he put on his tool belt, and his eyes met mine when I stepped onto the back porch. Immanuel's eyes were still a little upset, red around the inside like he had been crying, but he smiled.

"You should smile more. It fits you," I said.

"My job is not always easy. Not just any human could do it," he said, securing his belt around his waist. "Hi, John."

"Nice to see you again." I reached out, and we shook hands as he wiped his face and removed that last evidence of a sad disposition.

"I will be working the skinning post and rebuilding a better one. You will be spending much time here in the future," he said while adjusting his tools. "Papa will be here in just a minute. He asked for you to get your gun. And follow him," he said. I remained quiet. "There is a time for war and a time for peace. Your time for war is coming to an end. After this, your time for peace will be established until you come and stay with us forever."

"Sounds like what I want," I said with crossed arms.

"Get your gun," Immanuel said. His words were like nothing I have ever heard him say. I turned and went back inside to the fireplace without saying anything. I reached and took the M1, and slid the bolt back to check. The gun was ready. I grabbed a few extra-loaded clips and placed them in the pouch of my jacket, and returned to find Immanuel and Papa talking just outside the gate near the skinning post; I saw them put their heads together in agreement. Papa looked more powerful than ever.

"Follow him, and don't forget about Henry when the shooting starts. He ate the bread and drank the wine faster than you did," Immanuel said as he began to work on his project for the day.

Papa turned and waited on me. His face shined in the sun. I stood in front of him at the gate, and the chase began, due east, almost one-hundred-fifty yards right into a wall of American holly bushes that made us stop. Papa got low on the ground and went right underneath them. I followed, crawling on my belly for several feet. I eventually stood up and could see reasonably well inside the forest but almost slipped and fell into a dry creek bed. The drop was just over six feet deep, enough to twist your ankle good from the fall or to slip around quietly in the forest without being seen. I noticed that first.

I turned back to where I came from and could not see anything, not even the house. Nothing but a wall of thorns, red berries, and green leaves. Papa went in and out several times, showing me how to get under bushes quickly. I knew that this place would be beneficial to the coming battle.

The lion nudged me with his head, and I returned the love with a scratch behind his ear. Papa turned and jumped down into the dry creek bed.

"Wait, let me try something." I crawled back under the bushes, careful not to get poked in the eye by a twig. I searched for a faster way under the brush. I stood up and thought, how can I get under here quicker from the outside?

"I am going to try something." I took a few steps back, "I used to steal a base in baseball. It has been a while." I put the rifle on my back and just went for it, straight forward and headfirst under the bush. I cleared it but rolled right down into the dry creek bed and somehow landed on my feet. I lost my extra ammo out of my pocket somewhere. When I got my balance, Papa was looking at me. I stood up and saw my ammo clip in some leaves not far from me. I put it back securely, this time in my pocket. "Been a while." I laughed, and so did the lion once I turned my back. "I heard that."

Papa jumped down into the creek bed with me and slowly began to creep. A leaf did not crunch as I followed right behind him to learn how I could use this place in a fight. The creek bed was just low enough that when I walked, standing straight up, I could look and see the forest floor at eye level. Again, the wall of American holly bushes followed the dry creek bed. I could see under them with ease. This was an ideal setup for a fight.

"Papa, hold on." Again, with the rifle on my back, I crawled out of the creek and under the Holly bushes to a new world it seemed, oak trees, pine trees. Papa was below me, and I could not see him.

I walked along with the holly bushes for a bit.

"I cannot see the creek bed."

The holly bushes continued the whole way down, bending and twisting with the creek.

"The creek bed is perfect for a fight," I said, softly, as the ruffle of leaves could be heard, and the sound of feet hitting earth made me squat down. The noise became a little louder, almost a gallop, and from behind the trees to my right, a herd of wild hogs of mixed colors came running and stopped just in front of me and started eating acorns. I froze as the pack paralleled the holly bushes in front of me thirty yards or so. I slowly took the safety off of my rifle. The hogs were unaware of my presence as some flicked their tales. A few looked around as the others fed quickly. I pointed a big one out of the herd. I raised my rifle, just fixing to pull the trigger.

A mighty paw reached under the holly bushes and snatched a pig into the dry creek bed. The squeal shook the forest as hell broke loose. I fired my weapon, striking a medium-sized hog in the neck and dropping it instantly. My next several rounds hit the air and random objects due to my query's mass confusion and quick feet. The next round hit a giant pig, killing it quickly. My heart was beating fast. I had forgotten the thrill of an ambush.

When the forest became quiet again, I crawled back under the holly bushes and down into the dry creek bed to see what Papa had killed.

"Dang. Next time-kill something a little bigger," I laughed. The hog was solid black, and Papa wasted no time as he began to eat his kill. He grabbed his kill as I talked and carried it further down the creek bed to be alone. "Well, I guess the lesson is over with." I laughed and jumped out of the creek bed, crawled under the wall of American holly bushes and collected my kills, and began the adventure back to the farm, dragging the hogs behind me on the ground.

When I reached the farm, I was winded but not like I thought I would have been. Immanuel had run electricity from the shop to the skinning post and added an electric hoist. "No more scary hand crank. Now it's electric," he said and grinned.

"I was only gone a few hours, and the farm jumps ahead thirty years in technology," I said as I gave my friend a hug.

"Almost done. Just need to check my wiring," he said, getting some black tape from his tool bag.

"Cool," I said. My mouth was dry.

"Papa showed you the creek bed?" Immanuel asked.

"Yeah, if I can get there first, I will at least get a few." I paused and cleared my throat. "I really don't want to do this."

Immanuel quit fidgeting with the wires briefly. "Usually the things you do not want to do, you need to do," he said politely.

"John, do you want some water?" Mamaw asked from the front porch turning my attention toward her.

"Yes, please." I made my way to the porch to get it, placed my rifle on the back patio table, and went inside.

"Your package came while you were out with Papa, just over there," she said and pointed to the living room. There, I saw a large box at the front door that I opened, inside was more ammo and lots of it for my M1 and a nice ammo belt. The knot in my stomach grew more assertive. There was no denying that I had a fight coming now. That I was going to have to kill again.

CHAPTER 16

heard a car door slam, one and then two doors. "Who is that?" Mamaw asked while she washed dishes.

"The police are here," I said from the living room couch.

Mamaw ran and hid in the closet and managed to knock over a few cans of something and tried to wedge her big frame into a small area. "I am outside in the garden. Unpaid parking tickets!" she said just before the door closed.

I laughed and was not surprised by her actions as the two officers began to knock on the front door. I waited for a moment to let the noise in the closet settle down, but not before Mamaw farted out of nervousness.

"Do not be anxious for nothing," I said before she reminded me that we would talk about this later. "Ok, I will keep them in the living room, but you might as well come out of that closet." I waited patiently.

"Fine," she said, as the police knocked again. She abandoned her closet idea and went back to the kitchen. I had my hand on the front door handle and waited for her to clear the room before I opened the front door.

"John Hunt?" the officer asked.

"Yes, sir," I replied kindly and welcomed our guests.

"Sheriff Taylor and this is my Deputy," he said, then adjusted his belt while he shifted paperwork under his arm.

"Edward." That was all the deputy said. He was a little guy who did not fit; he was petite in size and strength.

"You don't come across to me as a police officer," I said.

"I like the challenge," the deputy replied quickly.

"Well, come on in and take a seat. Do you need anything? Coffee?" I asked.

"Coffee! Maybe some of that famous pecan pie," the Sheriff said as I went to get their request from the kitchen. I hoped the lion would be there waiting for me. I glanced at the spot where I first saw him while pouring our guests coffee.

"Where is your Mamaw?" the deputy asked. I looked her in the eyes and smiled in the kitchen as she handed me a plate of pecan pie and quietly ushered me out. I was reminded that there were guests in the living room.

"We will talk about her in a second," I said. I was very confident I could work this situation out as I took my seat. "Sheriff, why are you here? I know it was not for the pecan pie?"

The Sheriff thanked me and then threw a file on the coffee table labeled John Hunt. "We are not here over some dumb parking tickets. I will throw them out when I get back to the office," he said. His gray hair was uncombed when he took off his hat.

"John, we need your help." The deputy spoke up.

"My help?" I sat up in the chair in a more severe manner. "What made you think of me?" I asked.

"In a small town, word travels fast," the Sheriff said.

"And?" I replied with shrugged shoulders.

"Well, my nephew did some research and made some phone calls. Okay, he made a lot of phone calls, and we want you to volunteer some of your time. According to your military file, you are qualified."

"Sheriff, permission to speak freely?" I asked, knowing that my following few words were going to hurt. "I'm blunt when it comes to addressing a problem," I added.

"Okay, go on," he replied and set his coffee cup down.

"You are too old. You sat back in your comfortable position and didn't prepare for trouble. You should have retired. You are carrying a six-shot revolver in a world where everyone else has semi-automatic pistols that hold fifteen rounds. This nephew of yours was hired because he was your nephew. He's five feet tall and one-hundred-thirty pounds. Do I need to keep going?" I asked politely.

"No, that's fine," the Sheriff replied. "I know, I know!"

"You think you have a clue?" Edward interrupted and tried to pick a fight.

"Boy, shut up," the Sheriff said and pulled some lint from his shirt. "John is right! Retirement is just right around the corner and…"

"Enough." I held my hand up calmly. "You are sugar coating a request. Why are you here?" I asked again.

The Sheriff paused, then revealed a badge and slid it to me on the coffee table. "I had a deputy lose an eye last week. Some of these guys with families are just volunteering." The Sheriff paused briefly. "With your skills, I think I can swear you in right now." The Sheriff gave me a minute to process everything. I had never thought about working in law enforcement.

"I was hoping you would consider at least volunteering some of your time. But I think you are a great fit for this career," the Sheriff said. I noticed the Sheriff's eyes were focused somewhere over the fireplace and I turned in my chair to see. "I always wanted one of those, and I haven't fired an M1 in thirty years; since I left the marine corps." He turned to face his nephew Edward. "Now, that is a man killer! We had confirmed kills at almost a thousand yards in Korea. It's a powerful weapon!" The Sheriff's eyes gleamed.

"I can at least volunteer my time in some way," I said.

The Sheriff grabbed his hat and set the coffee cup beside the badge on the table. "I'll pick you up tomorrow morning, and you can keep that badge here," the Sheriff said. His nephew made quick haste to follow his uncle to the front door. "I will take care of your Mamaw's citations. Oh, one other thing, John," he said on the threshold of the front door.

"Yes?" I asked, still seated.

"There is a gap in your file after you left the service. You just disappeared. Where did you go? What did you do for work?" he asked as I joined them at the door.

I scratched my beard and thought about how I could respond. "Sheriff, do you like to hunt deer?" I asked.

"Yes, I got me a big one this past season!" He said while digging in his wallet and retrieving a picture to brag about. "Ten points!" he said, then smiled.

"Have you ever hunted a man?" I asked.

"No?" he answered, but seemed confused.

"If you ever hunted a man, you wouldn't waste your time on some stupid deer," I said with a grin as his jaw dropped to the ground. The two officers stared at me and finally turned and began to walk back to their patrol car.

The nephew mumbled as the Sheriff took the passenger side and climbed in rather quickly. The deputy hesitated and caught a glance of something in the backyard and held the door open to his patrol car.

"Come on, boy, we have tickets to tear up." The Sheriff reached for a can of tobacco.

"John, is that your dog?" the deputy asked, leaving the security of the patrol car and walking around the house's edge, and disappearing. I stepped outside to see what he was talking about and walked past the patrol car.

"Tell him to hurry, son," the Sheriff said. I nodded but eased around the corner of the house, slowly peaked to see the deputy had kneeled down beside Santo. My heart sank at what I saw. My beloved sidekick was lifeless on the ground. The deputy stood up and turned to me.

"There are multiple footprints headed towards that tall grass just past that fence," he said while he pointed.

"Deputy, get back here!" I yelled before I heard the shot and saw the smoke trail pass through the deputy's chest. He hit the ground hard and gasped for air. Bullets from the tall grass were like bees and struck the side of the house I had used for cover. The air became a cloud of brick, dirt, and wood instantly.

"Man down!" I yelled and ran to the front door to gather my M1 and ammo belt. I left the Sheriff to figure this out for himself. He frantically reached for the police radio when I could hear the bullets impact the side of his patrol car.

"John, what is all noise?" Mamaw met me at the door as the sound of gunfire grew.

"Get inside all the way, stay away from the windows," I said. I ran to the fireplace and loaded up my rifle, and grabbed my ammo belt as bullets began to pass through the windows and struck the pictures on the wall and shattered them into pieces. The air was filled with bits of wood.

"All my precious china!" Mamaw said as her dishes crumbled into a thousand pieces.

"Stay down, get to your room, stay low!" I yelled.

"What are you talking about? Stay low, crawl on all fours! You're crazy as hell!" she said as the bullets passed through the house. She just walked right through the gunfire and went to her room. She was unaware that Santo and the deputy had died just outside. I stood in front of the fireplace, knowing that it would block any bullets coming through the home. I could see the patrol car from there, and it was being shot up. The windshield looked like a piece of Swiss cheese as the bullets from the tall grass hit with furious wrath. The Sheriff stumbled out of the passenger side door with a bloody shoulder. The radio cord was stretched to the fullest as he tried to take cover behind the engine block and relay on the radio what had happened.

"Mamaw!" I yelled in the quiet.

"I am okay, just halfway under this bed," she said.

"Stay there!" I yelled back and tried to make sense of my next move. I heard the back door open beside the kitchen. I spun around the edge of the living room wall to see a man I did not recognize. That was all I needed. I was much faster than he was, and our eyes met for a split second. The M1's trigger was crisp. I put two bullets in his chest at fifteen feet, blowing him back outside; a mist of blood hung in the air. He hit the concrete lifelessly, only a twitch of the foot as the smoke cleared. My heart raced as I scanned the background of the south side of the house. The livestock had been executed. Mamaw's cattle laid lifeless in the field as the smoke from something burning blew past the back door.

"Something is burning! Are my pies out of the oven?" she asked.

"Stay in the bedroom!" I yelled as the sirens from the highway had gotten closer. I welcomed their approach. From my vantage point, I could hold off anyone that came into the house. I adjusted my ammo belt. I could see the tall grass from inside the farmhouse but not very clearly, a hundred yards away or so.

---- -- --

"Lycan! John killed Mississippi! He is lying on the concrete there. We have to go and get him," Henry, the one whom Papa loved, replied. I could hear their conversation from inside the farmhouse. "This was supposed to be a recon mission, but now we are shooting deputies, livestock, destroying a farmhouse, and we are setting a shop on fire.

"Silence, you should be grateful that Mississippi met with John Hunt. The rest of us can get more money. So run along into that farmhouse and say hello!" Lycan's Russian accent was intense, almost like a growl when he spoke. "The next thing we set on fire will be his home with everyone inside." Lycan looked Henry in the eyes and wanted a reason to kill him.

"I don't like this. We shot John's dog!" Henry said.

"Who cares? Next, I will kill the old woman." Lycan shrugged his shoulders and pushed some grass away from his face.

"I am Cherokee from the lost people of the plains! I will take the scalp of John Hunt and make my people proud, bringing honor to my name." Cherokee stood up and held his tomahawk and waved it in the air.

"You keep standing up like that, and John will put a bullet through your chest!" Henry said.

"I have the traps set, Lycan. If the police come out here to fight us. It will be like shooting fish in a barrel," the engineer said and twirled some type of fuse in his hand.

"John will come for us eventually," Lycan said. "He will not just sit in one spot; it is not his nature."

"I hear sirens! A bunch of police are coming over the hill, Lycan!" someone said with laughter.

"Find a way to flank the police upon arrival! Put some more bullets into that police car. I see life in that officer there," Lycan shouted as his men fired upon Sheriff Taylor's patrol car again. "John is still in the house. Prepare to smoke John out and kill the old woman if she runs," Lycan said before he fired his carbine.

"You didn't tell us much about this contract," Henry said as Lycan stopped firing his carbine.

Lycan lunged, put his hand around Henry's throat, and choked him.

"I am in charge here. If you do not like it, go up there and talk to John. Maybe he will kill you quickly. Or tie you to the skinning post over there and skin you like he did my business partner in Mexico." Lycan eventually let go of Henry's neck. Henry shoved Lycan while he coughed and moved down the line to distance himself.

– – – –

A few bullets struck the wall beside me again. The police sirens were a welcomed sound as I once again told Mamaw to stay in her room and hide. I moved and tried to glance out the broken front window to check on the Sheriff. He was face down on the bloody concrete driveway, lifeless. His eyes looked directly back toward me. I wanted him to blink. "Lycan, you're a dead man!"

I ran out of the front door toward the Sheriff, who held his bloody radio. I checked his pulse.

"This is John Hunt. Both of your officers are down," I said.

"Units are approaching now." The dispatcher said as a half dozen cop cars raced down the driveway. I turned the Sheriff over and began to administer chest compressions as blood pumped out of his mouth like a fountain. I rechecked his pulse as the police cars began to take immediate fire upon arrival. Men screamed as bullets hit like baseball bats against their police cars. I waved several men to me and used the house as cover.

"Oh god, the sheriff is dead!" I heard an officer yell.

I stood up and waved again as the bullets pushed me back down.

"Get over here!" I said from behind cover as men followed my command, the M1 slung on my back.

"Who is in charge here?" I asked with no response as another officer lay dead by his patrol car.

"We have to try and flank them. We will use that tree line there. There is a creek bed just inside those bushes. We can use it for cover and move around behind them. I killed one already," I said. I remembered the vantage points Papa showed me.

"We only have our service pistols," an officer's voice trembled.

"My Mamaw is inside. Get her in a patrol car now and get her out of here!" I said, before bolting toward the creek bed and running into a wall of bullets that hissed past me. I ran as hard as I could and passed the bodies of deputy Edward and Santo into the open pasture. The dirt exploded all around me as the bullets just missed their mark. An officer followed me, but he was cut down. Like Papa showed me, I slid under the American Holly bushes, held my rifle close, and rolled right down into the creek bed as the limbs above me exploded by the impact of bullets.

I checked myself for wounds, adjusted my ammo pouch, and began to make my way down the creek bed as the bullets hissed overhead. I knew Lycan would send his men into the woods to find me as a blue jay and then a crow in the distance gave an alarming sound.

I crept slowly as I could hear the gunfire from the farmhouse start back up again. A bird flushed again and a twig snapped. This time the bird was much closer. The American Holly bushes paralleled the creek bank and presented me with a wall of cover. Just the right height to look under from the creek bed, being that I was below my surroundings. From the bottom of the creek bed, I heard movement. When I slowly stood up to take a peak, a set of black boots was within reaching distance.

I grabbed the feet, not knowing who I held. But pulled them down into that creek bed for a fight. He reached for me quickly as we both fell to the ground. He swung with a fist and missed as I countered and knocked him down. I assumed he dropped his weapon on the creek bank above us. He reached for his knife, then tomahawk. He tried to close the distance, but again, I was quicker. With the butt of my rifle, I knocked him senseless, which allowed me the chance to get on top of him and snap his neck. His body still twitched as I put his tomahawk and knife in my belt.

I heard the shuffle of feet behind me on top of the creek bank.

"Where are you?" Someone said quietly. "Dallas, Dallas!"

I saw a single set of feet that crept slowly. He started to make his way toward my location. My pulse quickened.

"Dallas, where you at?" he whispered. The man was within ten feet of me but could not see me due to the wall of vegetation and my vantage point. "Dallas," he whispered and kneeled down to part the bushes, and my knife stuck him right in the throat, and I pulled him down into that creek bed and finished him.

The bullets kicked up dirt nearby. I paused to clean my face. The bushes parted several yards down, and a body rolled down the steep bank. The man eventually stood and coughed as bullets pierced the air above our heads. I waited for him to look me in the eyes.

"Hi, John," he said, and presented empty hands without a weapon and turned to face me, his rifle slung across his back.

"Bye Steven."

I shot the engineer in the chest and put another bullet in him after running past his body. I moved down further in the creek bed. I hoped I could flank Lycan and the rest of his team as the gunfire at the farm had stopped.

"John!" Lycan yelled. "We know you have a woman now. A pretty thing, she is. I think I will take her back with me." He tried to draw me out. "I can sell her to a pimp in the Middle East for a hundred grand. When he is through with her, I will sell her back to you for a dollar."

I slammed my fist into the dirt and pulled a root from the earth to keep from yelling out promises of pain. The bank above me exploded, and my ears rang as dirt rained down upon my head. I stumbled and moved further down the creek bed as my equilibrium was not balanced.

"Throw another grenade!" Lycan yelled from above. The explosion this time was in front of me. I had time to dive behind a fallen log for cover as the grenade exploded and shook the ground. I moved, and I hid in the darkness of the creek bank as grenades were tossed blindly by Lycan and his men.

"I will take the scalp of John Hunt!" Cherokee yelled and held his tomahawk as Lycan hid behind some debris in the shadows of the forest.

I stood to my feet and stuck my rifle through the bushes, and fired. I saw the head of Cherokee explode like a pumpkin; his body fell.

"Hey, Lycan! Cherokee isn't worth a dollar anymore!" I yelled before the gunfire started again. I ran further down the creek bed, as hard as I could to create distance between us.

"Flush him out like a deer! Bring me John alive or dead now, or none of you are getting paid," Lycan demanded from somewhere above as the sound of boots grew closer, like wasps. My heart raced as I was being cornered. Men began to stir like the wind all around me. Some hollered and whistled in confidence. I leaned against the wet dirt of the creek bank and disappeared.

Suddenly, a shadow slowly appeared above me as dirt fell at my feet.

"Lycan!" The figure above me yelled. "I found a dry creek bed."

"You men there, move forward," Lycan ordered from a concealed position.

"I found Dallas," someone said, as the evidence of my previous work was being discovered. One by one, I heard men slide down the creek bank into the creek bed with me.

"Henry, check for more bodies," Lycan said from up top somewhere.

My heart pounded in my chest. The figure above me slid down the bank and landed at my feet. The man knew I was there, slowly he turned to face me. The barrel of my M1 was on his chest.

"Henry!" Lycan said from above. "Any signs of John?"

I waited to test his loyalty. "Nothing here! His tracks must not have made it this far. I will check in the direction of the farmhouse. He might have abandoned this position altogether. You did mention selling his woman."

"Damn," Lycan said as I heard him finally begin to move closer, the leaves crunched under his boot as his shadow grew near. "Strip the dead of their gear! We are moving out."

My finger was ready to touch the trigger.

"Don't you move. Get your men away from my farmhouse," I said quietly.

"I see tracks going south," Henry yelled and looked up at Lycan on the creek bank as I hid in the shadows. The men abandoned the creek bed, moved north, pushed the bushes aside, and disappeared with Lycan.

"Where is Lycan going?" I whispered.

"We parked on the road, at an oil well or something, about half a mile from here. That is where Lycan and the men are going," he replied quietly.

"Did you kill my dog?" I asked.

"No! Cherokee killed the dog," he replied and shook his head.

"Who killed the police officers?"

"I didn't kill anybody. Lycan and I almost got in a fight over that," he stated his innocence, as I thought about what to do with him.

"Drop your weapon and your gear. Do not ever pick it up again. Follow the creek bed back to the farm and turn yourself into the police. Once we have proven your innocence of not killing a police officer, then come and stay at the farm," I said.

"Why would I risk a life in prison to come back and stay on a farm?" Henry asked as thunder roared in the distance.

"Because the one that gave you bread and wine, the little Hispanic guy, he works there. Papa wants to talk to you," I said and Henry stripped his gear in a heartbeat and ran toward the farmhouse. His hands held up in surrender.

CHAPTER 17

caught up to Lycan and the other two men about a quarter-mile from their vehicles. The rain fell hard enough to make it difficult to see my sights on my rifle. I laid ready for an ambush on a small pipeline, just big enough for a vehicle to pass through with thick brush on opposite sides. A twig snapped that startled a bird overhead. The bushes opened. I squeezed the trigger, and my bullet found its target. A man screamed in pain as he was left to defend himself as he lay on the ground in the open. I wiped the rain from my face and fired quickly as a man jumped across the path, and I missed. I was forced to take cover and reload my weapon. As bullets impacted the trees in front of me, dirt rained down on my head.

I saw the wounded man reach out to his partners who crossed the path but left him there to die.

"We will not expose ourselves to John's rifle. This man is gut-shot. Leave him. There is no honor amongst us thieves and murderers." Lycan grabbed the last man and left.

"Don't y'all leave me here to die like this!" the wounded man pleaded. He held his stomach and crawled toward some cover while coughing up blood. "Momma!" he cried. I knew he had only minutes to live, and I left him there to scream.

Meanwhile, Lycan and the last man preceded to make a hasty re-treat to their Land Rovers parked at an oil well location a half a mile through the woods. I knew of a shortcut I had found in my spare time weeks before this day. I crossed a small creek, then followed a game trail until I could hear the sound of a natural gas compressor on the oil well location. If I could beat them to their vehicles, I knew I could end this.

"John almost got all of us!" the last man faithful to Lycan said. They put their equipment in the vehicles. He slammed the doors in haste and cursed the rain.

"Lies!" Lycan snapped. "He got everyone but me," he said, before shooting his last man in the head and dragging him into the ditch. "I cannot come back with a survivor. Who would believe my lies?" Lycan said before he finished loading up his vehicle with his gear, and when he opened the driver's side door to make a quick exodus, I stood right in front of him as the rain dripped down from my face.

"You traveled many miles, Lycan, just to die," I said. Lycan slammed the door and distanced himself from the security of the Land Rover.

"If you just shoot me, we will never know who is the greatest amongst us, and you know the rules," he stated with a low growl. He circled around me slowly as I shot the ground by his feet to stop him.

"John, there's two-hundred-fifty-thousand dollars in that Land Rover. You can take it," Lycan said as he wiped the rain from his face.

"Guns?" I asked.

"Yes." His voice slithered like a snake. "You can take that girl and start a new life."

"There is no honor amongst us thieves and murderers," I said. As the rain poured and dripped from my forehead, I contemplated my deci-sion. But then, I had another thought.

"I was the best," I said before I killed Lycan right there with a single shot. I stood over him and emptied my rifle into his corpse as smoke filled the air.

– – – –

When John Hunt finished his story, he held an imaginary rifle in his hands. His eyes gleamed.

"What was in the Land Rover after you killed Lycan?" Paul asked John, as someone brought him some coffee. Paul's phone was ringing, he had several messages.

"Well, it was exactly like Lycan said. The money was there with more guns and some gold in the back. I took the Land Rover and left his body there for the buzzards," John said while yawning and looking towards his room. His eyes were red, and he rubbed them like a child that wanted to sleep.

"It is 4:30," Paul said.

"It is almost supper time for me." John smiled, reached out, and patted Paul on the leg.

"Well, I love the story," Paul said. John turned his wheelchair towards his room nearby and was gone. Paul politely put his chair back, discovered another random red Sharpie mark on his pants leg, and smiled. Paul checked on John before he left. The old man found the only shadow to hide beneath and slept in his room.

Paul thought about John's story as he drove home for the evening and assumed the thoughts of the story would stop with the business of being a dad and the chores that go along with it. He did not know what to do with the story. It wasn't until he was taking a shower that Saturday evening that Paul tried something he had not done in a while. Paul talked to God while rinsing the shampoo from his hair.

"God, what can I do with this story of the lion in the thicket?" Paul asked. He did not hear a lion roar or the ground shake. Just a loud thought in his head to write something down and see what happened.

"That seems stupid." Paul laughed.

Paul changed his clothes two or three times. He was nervous about this dinner with Miss Davenport and the rest of the employees at the steakhouse. He repeatedly told himself that this was not a date with Miss

Davenport, who waved Paul over to their table upon his arrival and had a chair beside her reserved for him.

"Hi, Paul," she said. She was dressed nicely and leaned in for a side hug. She smelled terrific.

Others stood up and shook Paul's hand from around the dinner table. Paul knew to dress well for a meet and greet.

"Thank you for having me," Paul said sincerely and adjusted his tie while still standing. "Thank you all for the invite tonight." Paul exposed a pacifier in his left pocket by accident which sparked laughter and a few jokes at the table. The wine had already been poured for several people.

"I will be your host for the evening," Paul said. "This is for sensitivity training," he joked, putting the pacifier in his mouth, and finally took his seat. The table of people clapped for his performance. The giggles eventually died down after a few minutes.

"Paul, what did you do before you came to work at one of the best nursing homes in the state of Texas?" a sophisticated woman wearing pearls asked.

"I was a distribution manager for Deepwater Oil and Gas company based out of Central Texas. Are you a board member for the nursing home?" Paul leaned forward in his seat.

"Yes, and other things for the community." She smiled politely.

"Wow, that is neat. If there is ever an opening—" Paul said before he was rudely cut off.

"What would make someone leave a well-paid job to become a maintenance man at a nursing home? You left what, a hundred thousand plus to make ten dollars an hour?"

Paul balled his fist under the table.

"Close," Paul replied with laughter. "It is fourteen an hour, and I left a hundred and fifty-eight thousand dollars a year. Actually, I was very good at my job." Paul hesitated but continued. "I just had to start over, not by choice."

"What happened?" Miss Davenport asked, holding a glass of wine. All eyes were on Paul as he fumbled with the pacifier in his pocket.

"Well." Paul bit his lip nervously. "There is no hiding it now." He cleared his throat. "My wife died giving birth to our son. I pretty much shut the whole world out to grieve. This is my first attempt to start over. To let go and meet new people." Paul glanced over at Miss Davenport. She put her hand on his, her eyes watering.

"That is the saddest thing." Miss Davenport smiled and stared at Paul.

"What have you been doing to help yourself move on?" another lady asked at the table.

Paul turned to speak to her directly and wondered in his chair.

"Not a lot. Something happened today. I listened to an old man tell me his life story and how he moved on. It was a very touching story. It challenged me in many ways. But I really do not know what to do with it." Paul shrugged his shoulders.

"Maybe you should write something down and see what happens," the lady replied.

The evening came to an end and the drive home was very peaceful. Later, Paul replied to several texts from Miss Davenport and others from the dinner before he shut everything down for bed.

Monday came and Paul began his first day on the job. He pulled into his parking spot, and it was an exciting time for Paul, who waved at everyone, greeting strangers with a smile along the way. He passed a security company working on those sliding doors that he was no longer afraid of. Paul waved at Miss Davenport, who was ready to smile back.

"Hey, are we still on for this Friday night?" she asked.

"Oh yeah." Paul grabbed the door handle to the maintenance office. "Good morning!" he said as Terry stuffed his face with a honeybun and Tylenol.

"Same here, not so loud," he said as the signs of a hangover were evident. "You can start today by trimming the bushes back on the property. The north side of the nursing home was growing pretty tall and thick." Terry pointed with his head leaned back and eyes closed.

"Wait, that's John Hunt's side. He loves the thick bushes that grow there," Paul pleaded for the sanity of an old man.

"He is no longer with us," Terry said.

"He died?" Paul stood to his feet about to go check for himself.

"Yes, he died! Got up after a year of not walking and walked out of here like something touched him miraculously. Then he stepped into those thick bushes and died right there. Somebody noticed a pair of shoes sticking out of the bushes," Terry exclaimed, throwing his hands up like a preacher.

"And another thing, this is also what happened over the weekend. Two other residents died in their sleep. Several others who could not walk just got up and walked this whole facility. They are being evaluated to be released. The deaf ears were opened, and blind eyes started seeing over the weekend. Five with cancer who were terminal are being checked out right now and going home. It's like God walked up and down these halls, touched doors, and healed people. There is an audio recording on the camera of a lion roaring. This place does not like change!"

Terry slapped his hand on the desk and almost cried. "I need a drink." Terry gnawed on his fingernails. "Oh, he left you something." Terry laid a letter with Paul's name on it, along with a journal on the desk. Paul leaned back in his seat and read the letter quietly.

Paul, we left you some bread and wine in the room. It is Imman-uel's best. I'm giving you my personal journal. I wrote down my time on the farm and my adventure with the lion in the thicket. This could be your guide in your pursuit of Heaven. I am with Papa now, and he wants to talk to you.
John Hunt.

"What does it say?" Terry asked.

Paul opened the front page of the journal and smiled. "The God that I know, April 3, 1979." Paul did not give attention to Terry, who constantly asked what the journal was about.

"Get those bushes trimmed," Terry said to Paul. Paul's head was in John's journal as he left the maintenance office.

Paul rushed down the hall just a short distance to find John's room cleaned, and the bed was stripped. Nothing of John's remained and the light was turned off. Not even a crumb or an empty wine glass could be found. Paul was aggravated and had hoped this letter really was an invitation to something bigger than himself. Paul moved the furniture around and looked for some evidence that the story he heard could possibly be true. He sat down frustrated and kicked a trash can.

"That is just my luck," Paul said and something caught his attention in the window, a flutter. The black butterfly had returned.

"That means something is about to change in your life, my friend."

Paul heard a familiar Spanish voice and turned to see a man carrying a basket.

"Hey," Paul said, looking this guy up and down curiously.

Immanuel smiled and set wine and bread on a table. "John has come home to stay with us." He smiled. "Papa is pleased with you, and your suffering will not be in vain, my friend."

"Immanuel?" Paul asked.

"Yes, we need God with us." He laughed, then spoke about traditions and why certain things must be done while neatly arranging the bread and wine on the table. He also said that Papa roamed the halls and called some of his people home over the weekend. Some, he healed, and others received joy and hope in their situation.

"We believe your heart is ready, and your suffering has prepared you for everything," Immanuel said while he motioned Paul to come closer to the table of bread and wine as they ate and drank in celebration of what was to come. "For the risks, you are about to take."

Immanuel touched Paul's forehead, and it felt like a bolt of lightning ran through his body. Immanuel began to tell Paul the secrets of Heaven, the great mysteries that scholars and philosophers have searched for but never found. Paul was instructed to reveal the unknown at the perfect time. So, please do not ask him.

Later that evening, in the comfort of his home, Paul opened his computer and wiped the dust from the screen. Paul knew the story of The lion in the Thicket but failed to experience his own adventure. The computer screen was blank for several evenings as he paced the halls of his home, rubbing his face and hands. Then, one evening, after the stress of the day was settled, Paul remembered the package with the name Papa on it in the pile of letters and gifts that were stacked a mile high on his kitchen table. Paul retrieved a pair of scissors and opened the box carefully. What happened then? Paul has yet to tell anyone. So, again, do not ask.

All I can say was Papa did send Paul closure and that his wife was safely in the arms of God. For several hours, Paul cried until midnight. He got up, put away several pictures of her from the house, and cried a little more. He even put her wine glass back in the cabinet.

Paul washed his face and returned to his computer with a cup of coffee. What he typed that night was the beginning of something extraordinary. The first chapter of his book could be described as one thing. It was a beautiful invitation.

CHAPTER 18

"Sir, can I help you?" The gentleman sipped a hot tea and stood in front of the glass display case.

"Yes! What is your final price on this ring here?" Paul asked as blood dripped onto the glass cover display, he wiped it up quickly as he could but failed to get all of it. "Final price! How much?" He tapped the glass and laid his wallet on the display. The man behind the counter handed Paul some more rags. "Thank you." Paul smiled and tried not to get any more blood on anything else.

"Sir, do we need to call an ambulance or give you a ride to the hospital?" the man asked, but kept his distance and reached for his cellphone.

"Ambulance? Is it that bad?" Paul laughed gently.

"You're bleeding all over my floor and display counters." The concern on the man's face was priceless. "Sir, you have a claw mark on your arm and face! Your pants leg is saturated in blood. It seems you have been attacked by a wild beast." The gentleman spoke so elegantly and revealed a first aid kit from under the counter.

Paul could not take his eyes off of the blue sapphire and diamonds. "That one there, that is the one, I will take that one." His finger pointed at his future; the man did not move fast enough and clutched a cellphone in his hand.

"Since I bled all over your store, I will pay full price. Do I need to call my bank to release the money?" Paul looked him directly in the eyes for the first time. Those eyes looked familiar. For a while, his own eyes looked just like that, almost dead. Paul had not seen those days lately and he felt concerned for this stranger. "I bet it is difficult, to see happy men spend money on someone they love, taking one of the biggest risks in life."

The man took a step back and after a moment, he spoke. "I can relate to that."

"Pain has a way of robbing us of joy." Paul smiled and paid for the ring with cash and a credit card. "I am going home to write about my own experience."

"When the book is done, I want to buy a copy." The man smiled and handed Paul his purchase. "What is it about, the book?" He leaned over the display counter, he seemed more comfortable.

Paul turned to face the man at the entrance of the store, the wounds from Papa started to hurt as the adrenaline wore off. The rag was saturated red and his heart was full. "It's about a lion."